SLOW TRAIN

THE SLIM HARDY MYSTERIES #4

JACK BENTON

AMMFA
PUBLISHING

BY JACK BENTON

The Man by the Sea

The Clockmaker's Secret

The Games Keeper

Slow Train

The Angler's Tale

Eight Days

SLOW TRAIN

1

THE TELEVISION HOST LEANED FORWARD. MANICURED nails and polished teeth glittered under studio lights which made Slim's head ache as badly as any hangover he could remember. He stared at her, concentrating on her eyes, the placid disinterest hidden inside decreasing circles of makeup.

'It's not the first time you've done what no one thought could be done, is it?'

Slim knew he would be sweating if the mentholated talcum powder pasted on to his face would have allowed it. As it was, only a single trickle ran down his back.

Not for the first time wishing he'd broken three straight weeks of sobriety with a drink at the bar across the street, Slim shrugged.

'I guess I asked questions that hadn't been asked before. The answers were just waiting there to be found.'

The host smiled a stunningly fake smile, more for the cameras than for Slim. 'Well, that takes nothing away from what you've achieved.' She turned to the audience, invisible beyond the glaring spotlights that angled in from left and right, leaving the space in between a haze of colour residue. 'Ladies and gentlemen, I give you, one more time, John "Slim" Hardy, private detective extraordinaire.' Then with another smirk, as though it would be the biggest scoop in the world, she added in a conspiratorial tone, as though it would stay between the two of them, and not be shared by however many were watching at home, 'Are you sure you won't tell us why they call you Slim?'

Including once backstage, it was the third time she had asked. Slim made the same reaction as he had to the other two: an awkward smile and a glance at the floor, followed by a stumbling, 'I wouldn't want to bore you. It's not a story worth telling.'

Then, apparently credits were rolling, applause that sounded recorded came from all around, and someone covered in microphones and wires had rushed forward to usher him off the studio stage. The host gave him a brief translucent smile, her gaze already far beyond this moment, thinking of next week's guests perhaps, and then he was surrounded finally by backstage gloom. People still buzzed around him, but he was able to make his way through the milling crowd of technicians, props people and other backroom staff, out into service corridors and back to a changing room where he was finally allowed a moment to himself.

He took a deep breath. If this was fame, he could do without it.

He was required to sign out at the TV company's front reception desk, but that was his only required interaction with anyone as he headed on foot back to the modest hotel the TV company had booked for him. The downstairs bar beckoned him like a forgiving ex-lover, but he managed to avoid its lure and head up to bed. Late at night was always the hardest, when the demons that were rarely far from his mind came out to play, but if he could get into bed without a drink he knew he would feel better in the morning.

His head still buzzed from the terror and thrill of the TV experience, but he was also exhausted after the studio had required his attendance from early this morning for screen testing, dress rehearsals, makeup, and other preparation. All that for a twenty-minute interview on his last case which he had mostly glossed over, reluctant to talk too much about events from which he had taken some months to recover.

The fame it had brought—as well as a decent court settlement which would keep him off the streets for a while —had provided its own form of reward. Now he was in demand, his old Nokia 3310, a near indestructible lump of basic phone technology, was ringing at all hours. Unsure who had been giving out his phone number, after some searching he had remembered the old website he'd started setting up and never finished.

Now he was renting a small office space in a pretty Staffordshire town, and had even employed an elderly lady called Kim to work as a secretary.

For the first time he was enjoying a level of success, but everything felt hollow. Even when he should have been chasing up a fraudulent insurance claim or rooting out an extramarital affair, oftentimes he'd find himself wandering aimlessly, unsure quite where he was heading or what he was doing, as though the success he had found wasn't really what he'd been searching for after all.

As he lay down to sleep he put the phone down on the table beside him but noticed a small box in the corner indicating a new voicemail.

Since changing his number, apart from a few old friends only Kim could reach him directly, so he picked up the phone and opened the message.

'Mr. Hardy, I hope the trip went well. I got an interesting call this evening, for a case I thought might be right up your street....'

Despite their high price tags, many of Slim's recent offers of business suggested a level of peril or trauma he was keen to do without. Families of murdered relatives wanting justice against acquitted killers, child abductions, gang hits gone wrong. He knew he wasn't helping his budding reputation as a man for the people by taking on only highly paid but safe fraud or infidelity cases, but it was doing his sanity a world of good.

However, as he listened to Kim's gentle monologue, he found himself intrigued. A historical missing persons case, dating back to the late seventies. Someone was looking for their mother, but unlike other cases he had been offered which he knew instinctively he would be unable to solve, there was something about the circumstances surrounding the disappearance that was different. It wasn't that it sounded easy—far from it—actually it sounded nigh on impossible. A literal case of vanished without trace.

As Slim wrote down the telephone number to call back in the morning, he knew now that he would struggle to sleep. The voicemail had already begun to fire within him the nervous excitement which made a case—for better or worse—hard to resist.

2

HOLDERGATE WAS A QUIET TOWN SET IN A WIDE, FLAT valley between two sets of hills in the middle of the Derbyshire Peak District. Getting off a bus a few stops outside the town, Slim walked the rest of the way through gentle, rolling farmland punctuated by attractive houses set at the end of long driveways and down meandering farm lanes.

Slim reached his lodgings, a guesthouse in a seventies-era building where the quietly spoken owner Wendy seemed surprised he had arrived without a car. His room had a view over the road, a left-facing one-way street lined by sycamores on both sides, the leafy branches obscuring a row of terraced houses and a single commercial property —a chip shop—half visible at the end. The bed was springy, the digital TV worked, the en suite bathroom was clean, and there were enough coffee sachets in a welcome tray for him to make one decent-strength cup.

He paid for a week in advance, thinking that the calm and isolation of the place might be nice even if he decided not to take on the case. He took a walk around outside, soaking up the quiet residential streets that slowly gave way to a few touristy shops and businesses clustered around a quaint church. The churchyard was well-mown and tidy, even the older graves clean and quite legible, offering no surprises. Across a street were a line of temporary stalls aimed at tourists; a burger van was sandwiched between an ice-cream seller and one selling local books and postcards.

The train station was a pretty stone building down a straight, slightly downhill road behind the church, lined on one side by a row of traditional stone houses. The road, straightened in the last forty years, continued over a level crossing; Holdergate Station itself was off to the right, set at the back of a small square bookended by a newsagent and a local branch of HSBC. The station front, with a stopping area for buses and taxis, was almost invisible through the trees of a leafy park which took up most of the area between it and the church.

Slim followed the road and climbed a set of steps to the station entrance. He bought a platform ticket for ten pence from a clerk who assumed he was a trainspotter, informing him that the next train wasn't due for another half hour. Slim told the man he just liked the atmosphere and took a seat on a wooden bench at the far end of the southbound platform. From here he had a view between a row of houses and a small village museum to the low hills of the Derbyshire Peak District. Holdergate was a sleepy place, one he found it hard to believe hid any dark secrets. Yet it was here on Saturday, January 15th, 1977, during a week of terrible blizzards, that a twin-carriage commuter train heading from Manchester Piccadilly to Sheffield had been delayed to a complete stop due to snow piled on the line, and a woman called Jennifer Evans had disappeared into thin air.

Slim looked at his watch. Just after a quarter to three. It was time.

He stood up, walked back along the platform, and went to meet the woman who had sent him an email, desperately begging for help.

3

'MR. HARDY, IT'S VERY GRACIOUS OF YOU TO MEET ME,' said the pepper-grey-haired lady who had introduced herself as Elena Trent. 'I didn't expect a return call.'

'I was intrigued by your case,' Slim said. 'I've never heard anything quite like it.'

They took seats across a table in a pretty cafe-restaurant called Porter Lounge, set in an old storehouse behind the church. The window looked up a gently curving main street with the hills of the Peak District just visible above the rooftops. Slim ordered a triple espresso—requesting one be specially made—and a cheddar cheese sandwich. Elena ordered a tomato soup.

'I've maintained all these years that she was abducted and most likely murdered,' Elena said, putting chubby hands on the tabletop and fidgeting her fingers as though struggling to control her nerves. 'I mean, it's always officially been treated as a missing persons case, but I don't think it ever was.'

'How old were you when your mother went missing?'

'I'd just turned twelve.'

Slim quickly estimated her as fifty-three, only six years older than he, although he had initially guessed her to be in her sixties. He watched as Elena's eyes dropped and her lower lip trembled. As she began to cry, Slim gave the server an awkward smile. The girl put the food trays down then hastily retreated.

'I sat up all night waiting for her to come home,' Elena said. 'But she never did.'

'Tell me in your own words what you remember of that night. I've read the files you sent me, but I'd like to hear it from you.'

Elena nodded, composing herself. 'My mother, Jennifer Evans, was on the eight-thirty commuter train back from Manchester after finishing work. She was a ward nurse at the Manchester Royal Infirmary. It had been snowing heavily all that day, and had continued into the evening. It was windy too, and the snow had drifted onto the line so badly that the train was held up at Holdergate Station. At that time we lived in Wentwood, the next stop up the line. There was set to be a delay of several hours, so she told me she was thinking of walking. It was only a few miles, and there was a footpath alongside the line in those days—an old bridleway—which was open enough for her to feel safe. She called me from a phone box outside the station and told me she was on her way. That's how I knew.' Elena wiped her eyes. 'But she never came home.'

'And no trace of her was ever found?'

'There was an investigation, but it came up with nothing. Her bag was found lying in a patch of grass a short distance along the footpath, but it wasn't discovered until three days later, once the snow had melted. The only other clue was the photograph of the footprints.'

Slim nodded. 'I remember you mentioned it in one of

9

your files and attached a copy.'

'Another passenger on the same train had wanted a photograph of the street outside blanketed in snow. He went to the waiting room window and lined up his shot. He told police that at the very moment he prepared to take his photo, a woman came into view. She walked a few steps up toward the park, then abruptly stopped and appeared to fall into the snow. The way the witness described it to police was that the woman scrabbled backward before immediately climbing to her feet, turning and running away in the direction of the footpath.'

'And he took the photo anyway?'

'Yes. He took the shot of the street showing my mother's tracks. He took the picture from inside the station building but told police he then went outside to look for her. The tracks, however, disappeared after reaching an overhang outside the station, and he figured she'd gone back onto the platform to wait. He thought nothing more of it until he saw a missing persons poster a couple of weeks later and recognised my mother as the woman he had seen.'

Slim frowned and scratched his chin. He had recently begun growing a little stubble to see what effect it had on clients, but had been dismayed to find most of it coming out as grey. He was only forty-seven but people told him he looked ten years older.

'So what do you think happened? Why the abrupt running off?'

Elena leaned forward. 'I think she saw someone watching her, and whoever it was scared her. She tried to get away, but later that same night she was abducted and murdered, and whoever killed her then disposed of her body.'

4

It was fair enough that Elena thought her mother had been murdered, but the few historic newspaper reports that Slim could find in the reference section of the local library were less sensational. There was a missing persons case, it seemed, but with no evidence at all beyond the bizarre behaviour witnessed by another passenger, the general consensus had been of an elopement with a secret lover. Sources close to the family claimed marital problems but didn't go into any details. He wrote down every name he could find and added any details of their relationship to Jennifer Evans, then gave each of them a rating out of five for how likely they were to A, talk, and B, offer any valuable insights. For a case nearly forty-two years old it was likely many of the witnesses and interviewees had died, and those alive today would have had their memories dogged by time.

It would be tough. Elena, controlled by emotions, would be unreliable, but she was still the closest person to the case barring the mysterious photographer who had taken the picture. His name was given nowhere in any news reports, and while Slim assumed it was a he, he realised there was no reference either to whether the photographer was even male or female, suggesting the information had been kept from the press.

Slim bought a coffee from a machine, then headed for a study area where he could use a computer with an internet connection. After a few minutes of searching, he uncovered the names of a couple of journalists who had covered the case. Further investigation came up with an obituary for one, but remarkably, the other was still active and working at a local publication called *The Peak District Chronicle* as sub-editor.

The *Chronicle*'s offices were a few miles east in Jennifer's hometown of Wentwood. Slim wrote down the address and then caught a little Peak District hopper bus from a stop outside the library.

The journey took less than half an hour. Slim, one of only three passengers—the other two an elderly lady and a teenage boy holding a skateboard across his knees—leaned against the window and stared out at the picturesque countryside as they bumped along country lanes, through rolling hills and open moorland, past pretty lakes and forested valleys. While it was certainly beautiful in a windswept, rugged way, Slim's detective mind couldn't think past it being a great place to hide a body.

Wentwood was of a similar size to Holdergate but a little more modern. Its high street had more cosmopolitan shops than its neighbour, but there were some pretty buildings around the quiet town square where Slim got off the bus. A clock high on the wall of a bank read just after three o'clock as he made his way up to the *Chronicle*'s offices. He had thought about calling ahead but wanted to have a better look around the local area, and he had also found that people were more likely to talk to him when you showed up in person. A phone call was far easier to refuse.

A receptionist took his request and headed off into a back room. Slim stared at pictures on the walls—a collection of nature-themed covers of the magazine, all depicting pretty landscapes of rolling hills. The subheadings on the covers were things like *Best Peak District Rivers for Swimming*, *The lost farming practices of the Iron Age*, and *Composting In 10 Easy Steps*. It looked like a peaceful line of work, one far removed from the supposedly crime-riddled wasteland of the surrounding industrial heartlands of Manchester and Sheffield.

'Mr. Hardy?'

Slim looked up at a grey-haired man in overlarge spectacles leaning through the doorway. He had a kindly face and wore a slightly tatty tweed jacket with a turned-up collar which made him look like he had just come in from a garden. His cheeks were rosy, his hair ruffled. He resembled a vet or a market gardener; it was hard to imagine him as a young twenty-something reporter covering a mysterious disappearance.

'Yes? Are you Mark Buckle? Thank you for your time. Please call me Slim.'

He felt awkward as he handed Buckle a business card with his name and contact details on one side and PRIVATE DETECTIVE written on the other. Kim had insisted he needed one, printing them off the computer on large sheets so they still had perforations along the sides. So far he had only given out three: two at the TV company and one to a police officer in the park across the street from his current flat in order to prove he wasn't homeless after the P.C. asked him to move on.

'I'm a private investigator looking into the

disappearance of a lady by the name of Jennifer Evans, way back in 1977. I was researching the case and came across a newspaper article you wrote. I know it was a long time ago, but I'd love to talk to you about it.'

Buckle frowned. 'Wow. Well, that was a long time ago. I've got to finish a few things up, but if you'd like to get a coffee after?'

Slim nodded. 'Sure.'

Buckle told him of a place where they could meet. Slim didn't feel like sitting alone while he waited, so he wandered up and down Wentwood's high street. A handful of cramped but modern chain stores rubbed shoulders with souvenir shops and local cafes. Slim peered in the doors of a tiny single-screen cinema, saw the film they were showing had been out six months already, and found himself smiling. If you were planning to disappear, the area was a good place to do it.

Mark Buckle was waiting at a table inside the window when he returned to the cafe.

'I thought you'd stood me up,' he said, standing up to shake Slim's hand. 'I quite often stop by here on the way home anyway, so I got in a doughnut.'

Unsure if Buckle was making a joke or not, Slim gave a noncommittal chuckle and sat down.

'I must apologise for the abruptness of my visit,' Slim said.

'Not at all. We're not exactly run off our feet over at the *Chronicle*.' He pushed the glasses up his nose as he gazed off into space, remembering old adventures, perhaps. 'So, it's Jennifer Evans you want to know about, is it?'

'Anything you remember. I was contacted by her daughter, Elena Trent. She wondered if I might be able to uncover what happened to her mother.'

'After all these years?'

Slim felt his cheeks redden. 'Mrs. Trent saw me on a, um, TV show. Contacted me on a whim, I think.'

'You're one of those TV detectives, are you?' Buckle said with a smile. 'Taking on impossible cases?'

'It's not like that,' Slim said. 'My last case was a little high profile, that's all.'

'Well, I'm not sure how much I can help you,' Buckle said. 'I do remember the case, though. I was a junior on my first contract and it was quite exciting to be asked to write about it. I'd never gone on location, interviewed witnesses, anything like that. For a time it felt like an adventure.'

'For a time?'

Buckle sighed. 'I lost my taste for it fairly quickly,' he said. 'I don't mean journalism, I mean crime reporting. In 1980 I got a chance to transfer to the rural affairs department and I've never looked back.'

'The Evans case turned you?'

Buckle laughed. 'Oh, that was nothing. No, a year later I had to cover the Strangler. I was done after that.'

5

JEREMY BETTELMAN. THE PEAK DISTRICT STRANGLER. Sentenced in March 1979 for the murders of four women whose bodies were found in the Peak District between January and April of 1978. Slim found himself in the kind of discussion he'd hoped to avoid by taking this case, about women found in ditches and shallow graves, strangled so violently that two of the four had had their necks broken. Bettelman had maintained his innocence throughout the trial, despite overwhelming evidence against him. Still maintaining his innocence, he had committed suicide in his prison cell in January 1984, taking whatever secrets he had to his grave.

Slim listened, wishing he had something harder to drink than coffee, as Buckle recounted the events of the long, terrible summer of 1978 from the point of view of a young journalist charged with covering an investigation for which he was far from qualified. Bettelman, arrested in June for one murder, had pleaded not guilty, even as first a second, then a third and fourth body were discovered over the next three months. Even as the trial began in August,

Bettelman refused to cooperate and maintained his innocence, the struggle for clear and damning evidence eventually dragging the trial out for more than six months. The whole region could barely look away during the trial, partly because of the chance he might be acquitted, and partly because of the fear that he was telling the truth and that the real strangler still stalked the streets.

'There was, of course, suspicion that Jennifer had been taken by the Strangler, but she fitted none of the victim profiles of the others. His victims had all been taken in the Greater Manchester area, had all been young prostitutes, killed locally and then dumped in the Peak District as though he was attempting to throw the police off the scent.'

He had eventually been picked up after his car had been recognised by a girl working the street. On searching the vehicle, police found fibres matching the clothing worn by three of the girls at the time of their deaths. He had been convicted of the fourth based on a boot print found in mud along a path a few metres from where the victim's body had been found.

Bettelman's defence had argued that the fabric could be explained by their client's regular use of working girls—something he never denied—and the boot print by the fact that he was also a keen hiker around the Peak District in his spare time.

In the end, his stated alibis had failed to add up and the jury had been convinced of his guilt. That there had been no such similar murders in the area in the four decades since suggested that the law had got its man, even though families of the victims hoping for a post-conviction confession had been left disappointed.

Buckle gave the kind of strained account of a man

haunted daily by what he had reported on, but remembered the events in vivid detail. Of the Evans case, unfortunately, he was less clear.

'It was one of those things I thought more on in retrospect,' he said. 'I was at the police press conference a couple of days after Jennifer's disappearance, and I did a little asking around of my own, as an eager young journalist was wont to do. There was really nothing concrete to go on. She never arrived home. Her bag was found lying alongside the old bridleway which followed the line between Holdergate and Wentwood. It wasn't found until the snow melted a few days later, so it was assumed to have been dropped on the night she went missing.'

'Wasn't there a witness?'

'Yes, that emerged a couple of weeks later. Someone had taken a photograph of tracks in the snow and apparently witnessed Jennifer running off in a supposedly panicked state.'

Slim nodded. 'There was no mention of a name in any of the reports I found. If I could speak to the witness directly, it would be a huge help.'

Buckle shrugged. 'I imagine you'll have to track down the official police report for that. The name was never given out to journalists because the witness was allegedly a minor, a young boy, only six or seven years old. The camera was an old Polaroid, given to him as a birthday present. He apparently spotted a missing persons picture in a supermarket window a few days later, told his parents, and they in turn told the police. Any statement he gave would have been in the presence of his parents. Plus, considering his age, his reliability as a genuine witness was always in question, therefore little was read into it. Trusting the imaginative mind of a child was likely to lead the police off on a wild goose chase. Sure, they had the photograph, but here's where the word "allegedly" takes centre stage. There's no absolute proof the boy saw Jennifer running away. There's no absolute proof he saw anyone at all.'

6

MARK BUCKLE LEFT CONTACT DETAILS, TELLING SLIM TO get back in touch if there was anything further he could do, but Slim felt like he had exhausted a good lead already.

Despite the lack of any decent connection, the Peak District Strangler was worth a read-up, so the next morning Slim woke early and headed for Holdergate's public library. He printed off a couple of web profiles and also checked out a couple of true crime books, even though he was sceptical of the sensationalist angle they usually took. Retiring to a study section, he looked over what material he had.

Born in 1947, Jeremy Bettelman had been a delivery driver for a local Manchester bathroom fittings firm. The nature of his job often required trips to Sheffield, which had come up in the trial as circumstantial evidence, giving him an opportunity to dispose of the bodies. Handed into the care of social services at a young age, he had shown many of the common traits shown by other serial killers: cruelty to animals, trouble with the law during his teenage years, violence and suspected abuse during his years in care, alcohol problems, a preference for being solitary. After serving two years for mugging two elderly women a month apart, it had seemed he had turned over a new leaf. He had trained in prison as an installer and gotten a job as a delivery driver as part of a new government rehabilitation program.

For six years, until being picked up and convicted as the Peak District Strangler, his record had been unblemished.

There were some who still believed him wrongly convicted, and that the real Peak District Strangler has been spooked by Bettelman's arrest and either gone to ground or relocated to continue his killing spree elsewhere, perhaps in a major metropolis like Birmingham or London where the deaths of a few women were more likely to pass unnoticed.

It was a can of worms Slim wasn't ready to open, but as Jennifer's disappearance had predated the murders by a full year, there was a strong possibility her abduction could have been a serial killer's prologue, a trial run, an attempt to understand himself, his desires, and his capabilities, before he settled into a routine which suited him best.

His eyes sore from a morning spent staring at various forms of text, Slim took his loaned books and headed out into the warm sunshine. A river threaded through the centre of Holdergate with part of the riverside turned into an attractive park. At one end, the railway line appeared through trees before cutting away to the station. Slim looked up at a hazy sun and wondered again how the most pleasant places could hold the darkest secrets.

He sat on a bench to have a sandwich and a coffee, pondering what ought to be his next move. He could follow up the possibility of Jennifer being an early victim of the Peak District Strangler, or he could consider other options.

No trace of her had ever been found, so the official line —that she had run off—might be the correct one. People did it all the time. Sometimes it was for the sake of a lover, or to escape an abusive spouse. Other times it was financial, escaping from bad business decisions, prosecution, creditors both legitimate and street. Then there were those who suffered from mental health issues, who might run away to escape demons only they could see, or even be unaware they had run away.

Then there were those who might quite literally have fallen down a hole.

Slim unfolded a map of the local area across his knees. The urbanised area had changed a lot, but the railway line and much of its surrounds remained unchanged.

Heading east from Holdergate to Wentwood, it made a gradual northward arc, curving around a small hillock called Parnell's Hill. Wentwood spread out around its northern edge, and Slim had marked with an X the location of the Evans' home, at the end of a long, straight street leading north from the station.

Officially, the distance from Holdergate to Wentwood was 3.2 miles along the bridleway that ran alongside, station to station. The Evans' house was another half a mile from the station, but Jennifer could have saved that by going off-road, cutting around the eastern edge of Parnell's Hill.

Crisscrossed by hiking trails according to the map, in the snow they might have been hard to follow, and in any case there was a far greater hazard than simply getting lost.

Parnell's Hill was quarry country.

7

WIND UNNOTICEABLE IN THE TOWN HAD MADE ITSELF FAR more apparent as Slim stood at the top of Parnell's Hill, gasping for breath from a strenuous climb to the lookout point. Figuring that a six-mile round trip was still a single digit number and therefore easily manageable during a warm afternoon, he had already decided to cut his losses and get the evening train back from Wentwood, the town's outer urban areas spread around the foot of the hill.

From here, as well as a panoramic visual feast of the Peak District, he could see the exact route Jennifer might have taken, following a signposted hiking trail that intersected with the bridleway and curved around Parnell's Hill's base.

He had taken that route himself, turning off halfway to climb to the summit. A pleasant, grassy trail had become a strenuous climb, but even on the lower path the danger was apparent. Winding amongst the remains of quarrying operations now reclaimed by local vegetation, there were dozens of rocky slopes, gullies, and crags.

Fun climbing for adventurous teenagers it might be,

but what about a final resting place for a woman who had tried to walk home in the snow and taken a wrong step at the precise wrong point?

Pausing on a bench to catch his breath, Slim pulled a sheet of paper out of his pocket and read the information he'd printed off from a historical weather records website. The snow on the day of Jennifer's disappearance had been forecast but come on heavier than expected. While it was likely, as a local person familiar with the area's weather, that Jennifer had been prepared for such weather conditions, she may have been keen to get home as quickly as possible. She might have been moving quickly, running even, increasing the risk of a deadly fall.

Slim climbed back down to the main path and spent some time peering into the gullies and cracks alongside the path. Some were marked only by a knee-high rope fence, one that would have been easy to miss in the estimated twenty centimetres of snow that had fallen that night.

A couple of times Slim even clambered carefully down over rocks the size of cars to reach grassy hollows hidden from the path, peering into shadowy spaces, pulling back shrubs and brambles in the search for cavities large enough to hold a body.

It wasn't that he hoped to find something, but he was examining the possibility that a body could have remained undiscovered.

According to the news reports, a series of searches for Jennifer had been undertaken over the following days. Even though they had found nothing except her bag, several major searches of the countryside, often involving hundreds of volunteers, had been undertaken while the Strangler was active. Two of the bodies had been found buried in shallow graves a couple of hundred metres from a major road.

Slim frowned and shook his head. It wasn't impossible that Jennifer's body had fallen somewhere and lain undiscovered for over forty years, but with no animal capable of dragging off a human corpse, it was highly unlikely.

Slim stood up and stared off into the distance. The tumbling slope flattened out, becoming an earthy chaos of slag heaps buried in bracken and brambles before the moorland took over once again.

Of course, she might have fallen but not died. She could have dragged herself through the snow, disorientated, her strength giving out far from the path.

Again, he shook his head. He couldn't rule it out, but there were definitely other possibilities which were far more likely.

With a shrug, he began the arduous climb back up to the hiking trail, leaving whatever secrets the old quarries held behind him.

8

'THANKS FOR AGREEING TO MEET WITH ME.'

The old man leaned on his stick and flapped his spare hand as though to swat a fly. 'Not a problem. Come on in. Excuse the mess. The home help doesn't come until tomorrow.' With a wink, he added, 'She just sits around drinking tea unless I leave her work to do.'

Slim followed the hobbling old man into a cluttered living room. Police memorabilia lined the shelves and hung from the walls. Slim noticed a couple of bravery awards and recognitions for exemplary service.

The old man offered Slim a chair then sat down in a special recliner, groaning as he slowly lowered himself into the seat, his cheeks reddening with the exertion.

'I'm afraid there's not much left of me these days,' he said.

Slim nodded at the nearest shelf, on which stood a couple of framed black and white photos of a young man in a police uniform, alongside a constable's helmet in a glass case, and a couple of mounted medals.

'Looks like you gave yourself to the Force,' he said.

'I was as dedicated as they come for nearly fifty years,' said the retired former Chief Inspector Charles Bosworth. 'It was everything to me.' He gave a phlegmy chuckle. 'The Force was my life. That's why I never married. She was my mistress.'

'It must have been hard to give it up.'

'They had to drag me out of that office,' Bosworth said with that same laugh. 'I stayed on in part as a consultant. And after that dried up, there was still the occasional visit by someone such as yourself wanting to know about a specific case. Jennifer Evans, wasn't it?'

'That's right,' Slim said. 'I'm a private investigator. My last couple of cases were somewhat … troublesome. Jennifer's case sounded a lot less dangerous, if you understand where I'm coming from. A forty-year-old mystery. No danger involved, and no risk, right? If no one's figured it out by now, there's little chance I could do any harm.' Slim looked down at his hands. 'I've found out the hard way that some mysteries should stay buried.'

Bosworth harrumphed, leaving Slim unsure whether he agreed or not, but he picked a couple of folders off a table beside him and handed them across.

'I remember Jennifer Evans,' he said. 'A mystery like that never leaves you without a certain kind of feeling. I mean, she appeared to vanish into thin air.'

'No one ever does that,' Slim said, recalling a previous case. 'They always go somewhere.'

'But finding out where is the tough part, isn't it?'

Slim opened the top file and flicked through the contents. Much of it was the same as that provided by Elena, but there was some additional material. Some photos of Jennifer, one in her nurse's uniform, another of her holding a young girl, a third with a man, he had never seen. She looked like a perfectly normal, happy mid-30s woman.

There were also transcripts of interviews undertaken with other passengers. Most were short—a page or less— with the passengers asserting they did not know Jennifer, nor did they see anything suspicious. One noted that she was known as "that pretty nurse who sometimes takes the late train", another that she "always had a smile", and a third that "she seemed to have no care in the world."

'After you contacted me, I got in touch with an old friend at Derbyshire Constabulary and asked for a copy of the file,' Bosworth said. 'I still have enough sway that I got it without question. However, I'm afraid there's not much to go on.'

'The tiniest clue could be important,' Slim said.

'Oh, no doubt, but remember, this was in the days before DNA testing was used for everything. And Jennifer's body has never been found. That's a huge elephant in the room.'

'May I ask what you thought happened to her? Off the record, if you like. Disregarding what the evidence might have suggested.'

Bosworth frowned. 'In the police we go on evidence only. I never had much use for idle speculation. Why don't you tell me what *you* think happened?' He smiled. 'And then I'll tell you why you're likely wrong.'

Slim rubbed his chin, tugging on a couple of days' of stubble. 'Well, she might have tried to get home on foot but wandered off the path.'

'Her body would have been found. There are a few holes around here and there, but nothing deep enough to not be searched.'

'Okay, perhaps she was abducted by the Peak District Strangler.'

Bosworth shook his head and gave a sad smile as though he were talking with an amateur.

'Of course we considered it, but Bettelman lived in Manchester. And even if he had been in Holdergate on a Saturday in January at that time of night, remember it was dumping with snow and had been for a couple of days before. Would he really have risked an abduction in those conditions? It would have been foolhardy in the extreme.'

'Then she ran away. Abandoned her family. She had a lover, or perhaps her husband was a monster behind closed doors.'

'Have you asked the daughter about that?'

'Not yet.'

'Well, I did, at the time. By all accounts they were a happy family. Her disappearance left her husband, Terry, distraught. He spent every weekend for months afterward combing the local area, convinced she had fallen on her way home. He found nothing, but the stress of it all took him to a nervous breakdown. He was in and out of hospitals, and Elena was shipped off to her grandparents in Leeds. He never did get over it, and died, something of a wreck, around 1990.'

'It sounds like you kept in touch.'

'In a professional capacity, yes. You see, the case was never officially closed until Jennifer was declared legally dead in 1997, twenty years after her disappearance. It was a case I kept open, always looking for new leads, but none ever came.'

'So what do you think happened?'

'I couldn't tell you precisely, because I'm not sure what it is, but I can feel in my heart that she's dead.'

'Why?'

'Because what woman planning to leave her family would call her daughter like that? Imagine the callousness required. This from a woman who worked as a nurse at Manchester Royal Infirmary. No, I'm certain something happened to her, but whatever it was happened after she had finished that final phone call.'

'So,' Slim said, 'what that boy saw is key.'

'I'm afraid so,' Bosworth said. 'We have nothing to go on but the memory of a six-year-old child and a single photograph of a few scuff marks in the snow.'

9

'DON?'

'Hey, Slim, you're sounding well,' said Donald Lane, an old friend of Slim's from the Armed Forces who now ran an intelligence consultancy in London. 'What can I help you with?'

'I need help tracking someone down.'

'Okay, sure. Still alive?'

'As far as I know.'

'That's a start. What else do you have?'

'He would be in the 48-50 age range. Grew up in Sheffield. First name was Toby. Some sort of creative career. An artist, maybe.'

'Well, I'll have a go, Slim, but that's a pretty vague outline.'

'That's all my contact could remember,' Slim said. 'As a boy he witnessed a possible crime, but as a man he sought to distance himself from it. That's what I was told.'

On the other end of the line, Don sighed. 'Well, it's not much, but I'll do what I can.'

'Thanks.'

Slim hung up. Next he called Kim.

'Good morning, Mr. Hardy. How is your investigation going?'

'Pretty dead end as usual,' Slim said. 'I'm afraid I've got some drudge work for you.'

'Well, that's what I'm here for.'

'I need you to dig up a staff list from Manchester Royal Infirmary circa 1977. I appreciate that some might be very old or passed on, but I'd like contact numbers for as many as possible.'

'I'll get to it.'

'Great. Only if you have time—'

Kim laughed. 'Mr. Hardy, you've never been a boss before, have you? Of course I'll have time. You pay me to have time.'

Slim smiled. 'It's a new experience for me, for sure.'

'I'll get back to you tomorrow.'

'Thanks.'

He hung up. Grabbing his jacket off the back of a chair, he hurried to another arranged meeting with Elena, over fish n' chips in a local restaurant. Elena had brought with her a box of mementoes belonging to her mother.

'I'm not sure if anything in this box will be useful,' Elena began. 'She wasn't one for material stuff. Neither was Dad. You know, we had furniture and things, pictures of family, but these were the only ornaments or other decorative items that I still have.'

Slim glanced into the box. A porcelain model house, small enough to balance on his palm. A bronze war medal. A small brooch in the shape of a swan. A few other items, all of which had the impression of being family keepsakes. Likely, none had any value to an investigation, but it never hurt to make sure.

'Can I borrow these?'

'Of course. Just, you know, be careful. They might look like nothing, but they have great value to me.'

'I understand.'

'Thank you. Have you—I mean, have you made much headway?'

Slim shook his head. 'I won't lie to you, Mrs. Trent. I don't think that would serve much purpose. At this point, I haven't the slightest clue what befell your mother.' At Elena's look of disappointment he added, 'However, I'm only a couple of days into the investigation. I've made some good contacts, and I'm confident there's a story to be uncovered.'

'Well, it's been forty-two years, so I suppose I can wait a few more days,' Elena said.

Slim forced a smile. He wanted to point out that the chances of finding her mother were remote, but he couldn't bring himself to dash her hopes so soon. Not until he'd followed up every possible lead.

'At the moment I'm just trying to cross off possibilities,' Slim said. 'The more I can eliminate, the more chance I have of discovering a lead which will reveal what happened.' He paused, watching Elena as she ate, not looking up. 'I'm sorry to have to ask this, but, as I say, I have to eliminate possibilities. Was there any reason why your mother might have wanted to run away?'

Elena looked momentarily shocked. She gave a shake of her upper body as though struck by a sudden chill breeze, before finding her composure again. When she looked up, Slim could tell just from her eyes that it was a question she had often considered.

'That I am aware of, there was no reason why my mother might have wanted to leave. We weren't a "tabloid family", if that's the right way to put it. My parents didn't have a perfect marriage, but it was pretty good by any standards. I was twelve, and aware of what was going on. There was tension when my dad got made redundant, some also when my mother took on extra shifts. But these were general things, and they sorted themselves out. My father got another job. My mother's hours went back to normal. Day-to-day stuff. They rarely even argued. I've thought about this a lot, and I used to wonder if my mother had a lover she ran away with. We were close, though. Why abandon me? Why all these years without a word? My father … he barely had a temper. He was no secret tyrant. If she wanted to leave him, he couldn't have done anything about it.'

Slim nodded. He made shapes on a notepad with a pen, wondering if there was anything useful he could write. 'Have you ever received unusual mail over the years?' he asked. 'Unsigned letters, Christmas cards, anything like that?'

Elena shook her head. 'I've always been suspicious of anything that I couldn't identify. But in the end, I always figured out who sent it.'

'Are there any … how could I say? Any shady characters in your family or your parents' friends circle? An uncle, perhaps, a jealous neighbour? Anyone who might have taken an unhealthy interest in your mother?'

Elena sighed. 'No one I can think of. Believe me, I've spent years thinking about this.'

'I can imagine. At this stage I don't have any decent leads, but, as far as I can see it, there are three options. One: she got lost on the route home and perished from exposure. Two: she was abducted shortly after making the phone call. And three: she took the opportunity given to

34

her by such freak weather conditions to run away and start a new life somewhere else.'

'And which do you think is most likely?'

'Well, in actual fact, all three can be written off,' Slim said. 'One, because her body or her remains would have certainly been found. Two, because the adverse weather would have made the risk factor too high, and three, because if that was her plan, why call you? And why wait until she was within walking distance of home? Why not just stay in Manchester after her shift, give herself a decent head start?'

'Are there any other options?'

Slim sighed. 'None that I can see at this point. May I ask, just for interest's sake, what do *you* think happened? What have you considered most likely all these years?'

Elena took a deep breath. 'All these years I've believed someone took her,' she said. 'She was born in Wentwood. She told me she used to play around the railway line, up and down Parnell's Hill. There's no way she could have got lost, even in the snow. And if she had left us for someone else, there's no way that she would have been silent all these years.' She gave a vehement shake of her head. 'No way. Impossible.'

Slim nodded. Elena had said it with such conviction he could almost believe it. But, like everything else, there was a lie to be found somewhere.

He just needed to overturn the right stone to find it.

10

THE PHONE BOX OUTSIDE HOLDERGATE STATION actually still stood, a classical old-fashioned red phone box on a corner right beside a taxi rank. The phone inside, however, no longer worked, with a sign taped to the shelf inside stating that passengers wishing to make a call should use a newer payphone inside the station.

Slim opened the door and went inside, trying to visualise how the street might have looked forty-two years ago. A turning circle outside the station could have sat four cars end to end. Three roads led off, a main road angling slightly uphill which was two lanes wide, then two smaller roads to the left and right. The left side road was a single lane which led along the tracks for a short distance, curving away into a residential cul-de-sac exactly where the bridleway began, while to the right the road was a dead end, ending at a steel gate that opened onto a goods yard, a sign beside the station indicating as such.

The buildings to either side were 1960s-era, and while they now housed a couple of mini-marts and a travel agent, Slim had seen in old photographs that one had once been a bank, the other a greengrocer's. Both would have been closed and shut up at the time the night train passed through on January 15th, 1977.

Up a slight hill leading directly away from the station was Holdergate Park. In front of the park, the road jack-knifed, continuing alongside the park to the crossroads where the church stood. A railing fence separated the park from the street, a line of trees giving it a shadowy overhang. Billboards, one advertising a soap powder and another a newly released Japanese car model, shone from a bus stop a little to the left. The same photographs had shown Slim that the bus stop had previously been on the right-hand side, outside the bank.

From the phone box, Jennifer would have been able to see as far as the park. Advancing up the street as far as the photograph of her footprints suggested would have allowed her to see farther into the park, and also a little up the road toward the church; however, as, according to police reports, it had been actively snowing at the time of her disappearance, not to mention dark, it was unrealistic that she could have seen farther than the park fence. Slim estimated that whatever she had seen to alarm her enough to change course had been within a semi-circle of about twenty metres.

It wasn't far, barely as far as the two buildings on either side of the square, or the park's fence to the north.

Slim frowned. Had she seen something through one of the windows? Something that had upset her enough to run off? Or perhaps she had seen someone in trouble and gone for help, only for an accident to befall her before she made it?

He went into the train station and called Kim, using

37

the new payphone rather than trusting the reception on his old Nokia.

'Hello, Mr. Hardy. How can I help? I should have that list of staff from Manchester Royal Infirmary by the end of the day.'

'Thanks, Kim, that's great. I have something else for you to do. If I give you a couple of addresses, do you think you could hunt down the occupants of the properties from 1977? I mean, they were commercial properties, but these places often have rented flats on the upper floors, and, well, it could be possible someone had come down in the night....'

He trailed off, aware of how clumsy and ridiculous his request sounded. Kim, however, didn't even pause to show her frustration.

'Read me the addresses to write down and I'll see what I can find,' she said. 'Have you got a computer set up down there?'

'Um, not yet. I'll get something sorted.'

'It would help a lot if you had an email I could use,' Kim said.

'Right. I'll get to it.' Slim felt awkward as he hung up. Kim had regularly insisted that he get a decent laptop with a roving WiFi signal. She had also wanted him to trade in the old Nokia for a decent smartphone, but he had stood firm on that.

As he got a coffee and sat down at a table overlooking the street outside, he wondered what chance he had of unravelling the mystery. Right now, it felt less than zero. Jennifer Evans had gone without leaving a trace.

Or had she?

11

'THAT'S RIGHT,' CHARLES BOSWORTH SAID. 'WE DID find her bag. It was dusted for fingerprints. However, the only ones found belonged to Jennifer herself. We were able to match them to those found on other personal items provided by her husband. The bag was open, and the clasp was broken. However, her purse was inside, untouched. The way the ice had frozen without affecting the contents made this clear. Quite high science for the time.'

'I read nothing about it in the newspaper reports.'

Charles Bosworth nodded. 'That's because, rightly or wrongly, we didn't consider it of importance.'

'But why not?'

Bosworth smiled. 'Let's see if you can figure that out, young Slim.'

'Are you testing me?'

Bosworth smiled. 'It might be interesting to see if you have the mettle for a case such as this. I've met a lot of private investigators over the years, and they were dilettantes, every last one. Here. Take a look. Tell me what happened.'

He pulled the copy of the case file out from a shelf under his coffee table and withdrew a file of photographs showing Jennifer Evans' bag and the items found inside.

The bag, closed with a snap clasp, had been opened. Parts of the leather had been scratched, a semi-circle of small depressions around the clasp area, some deeper than others.

Slim looked at the photographs of the contents. A small purse containing approximately seventeen pounds in used notes and coins. A hospital staff card. A local bus pass and a train commuter ticket. A lipstick and a pot of blusher. Half an opened pack of Wrigley's spearmint chewing gum. A pack of Lucky Strikes, with three cigarettes remaining.

And a torn piece of plastic wrap.

'That was found a couple of metres to the left,' Bosworth said. 'But it matched a smaller piece still inside the purse. Figured it out yet? No footprints.'

Slim looked up. 'A sandwich wrapper, isn't it?'

Bosworth gave a slight nod. 'The rest?'

Slim pointed at the picture of the bag. 'These depressions. They're teeth marks.'

Bosworth looked like the sun had just emerged from behind a cloud. 'There's something to you after all, Mr. Hardy. Tell me more.'

'No tracks because the bag was taken by an animal. The snow would have covered animal tracks quicker than it would a person's, particularly if a wind had been blowing. If the snow had blown into drifts deep enough to stop a train, it's safe to assume that it was.'

Bosworth nodded. 'We found small traces of processed ham. The animal would have smelled it and likely ripped the bag open. It also means it could have been picked up anywhere around the station area, at any time on the night in question.'

'Has the animal been identified?'

Bosworth shook his head. 'We believe it was a fox, and comparisons with a fox's jaws backed us up. The marks are approximately the size of a fox's jaw.'

'But it could have been a dog?'

Bosworth nodded. 'A small stray, possibly.'

Slim frowned. 'Do villages like Holdergate have a lot of stray dogs?'

'No, hence the belief that it was a fox.' Bosworth sighed. 'It was an interesting find, but unfortunately it came to nothing.'

'Do you still have the bag?'

Bosworth shook his head. 'I'm afraid not. After Jennifer was declared legally dead, the physical evidence was destroyed. We have just these photographs left.'

'A shame.' Slim looked up. 'I would really like to take a look at it.'

'I'm sure you could learn nothing more. It was thoroughly examined.'

Bosworth went to gather the photos, but Slim put a hand on the one showing the front of the bag. He looked up and their eyes met.

'I was in the army for nine years,' Slim said. 'We always had some dogs on the bases, pretty vicious things if you didn't know how to handle them.' He pointed at the depressions on the photograph. 'It's impossible to be sure without seeing the bag itself, but from the way these marks seem heavier on the outer side rather than the inner, it seems that this fox or dog had quite a battle to claim this bag.'

Bosworth rubbed his chin and frowned. He nodded slowly as he watched Slim, saying nothing.

'See, how it appears to me, this bag was wrestled out of someone's grip. I'm aware foxes are nervous creatures, so I don't know how desperate one would have to be to wrestle a bag out of a woman's hands.' He tapped the tabletop. 'Not unless she was already dead.'

12

'THEY TOLD ME ABOUT THE BAG,' ELENA SAID, SITTING in the cafe across from Slim. 'The investigation believed it was most likely found by a fox and dropped on the path after the food had been taken. It was like a little tease really, something but also nothing, if you know what I mean.'

Slim nodded. He hadn't told Elena his suspicions because it was not something he could prove, nor did he want to get her hopes up on something that was a tenuous clue at best.

From his bag he pulled out a sheet of paper and passed it across the table to Elena. 'My assistant came up with this list of staff from the Manchester Royal Infirmary around the time that your mother worked there.' Elena looked stunned, mirroring how Slim had felt when Kim faxed him the list.

'How did you get something like this?'

Slim smiled. 'I employ someone far brighter than me. Obviously it's been a long time, and many of these people will be elderly or may even have passed away. My intention

43

is to talk to as many as possible, but to save time I'd like you to have a look at these names and tell me if there are any whom you recognise, any you heard your mother mention, anyone who was a known friend.'

Elena frowned as she squinted at the list. Slim wondered how reliable her memory would be.

'Well,' she said, 'there were a couple of names I remember she mentioned … ah, here. Tim Bennett. He was a consultant on her ward. And this one, Majorie Clifford. I recall hearing my mother say her name on more than one occasion. It sounded like they were friends.' She looked up and shook her head. 'I'm sorry I can't be more helpful. It was a long time ago. And I was reaching that age, you know, where I talked to my mother as little as possible.'

Slim smiled. 'I'll be making my own enquiries in any case,' he said. 'I'll be in touch again as soon as I have anything to tell you.'

They parted outside the cafe, Elena lingering as Slim walked away, her reflection caught in the windows of a couple of shops he passed. He prayed he wasn't raising her hopes too much.

Back at his guesthouse, Slim went through the contacts he had acquired so far and sat down at a corner desk to begin making calls. Kim had done an incredible job in compiling information on Jennifer's work colleagues, but unfortunately so much time had passed that many possible leads were gone. Tim Bennett, for example, had died in 1994 at the age of 76. Marjorie Clifford, however, was possibly still alive, but Kim had only been able to locate a postal address. Slim had written her a letter, but he wasn't hopeful of a reply.

He was about to start making calls when his phone abruptly rang.

'Hey, Slim,' Donald Lane said. 'That person you were asking about? I think I've tracked him down.'

'Fantastic. Do you have any contact details?'

'Kind of. The guy's name is Tobin P. Firth.'

Slim frowned. 'That sounds vaguely familiar.'

'It would be if you had children, or if you if you spent much time in the book aisle in Tesco's. The guy's a bestselling children's author. He wrote the *Night Assassin* series. My daughter's a massive fan.'

Slim nodded, recalling the last time he had been in the supermarket and somehow wandered into the books section on the way to the frozen meals. A colourful stand had been advertising a new release in Firth's series.

'Did you get a contact number?'

'Only of his publicist. That was the best I could do. The guy's pretty famous, it seems.'

13

FOURTEEN BOOKS IN AN ONGOING SERIES. SLIM BOUGHT the first from the local bookshop and took it to an adjacent cafe to read.

Within a couple of pages he knew it wasn't going to be his thing: kids with magic powers fighting all manner of hideous fairytale creatures while running about a fantastical country on a quest for something Slim doubted he would read long enough to identify, but the coffee was too tepid to drink in one swallow so he snuggled down into a sofa seat and forced himself to read on.

According to the sign above the display, Firth was a "bestselling local author". A sticker on the front of the book took it up a level with "Sunday Times Bestseller", which even Slim understood meant the author had reached the upper echelons of literary society, at least where sales and profits were concerned.

Half an hour and two coffees later, Slim had decided once and for all that he wasn't a reader of children's books, although on a subjective level he could see why they were popular. The lead character was a girl called Claire Wilkins

46

who woke up one day with the ability to see nether creatures, whatever that meant, because the supporting cast was a series of oddball creatures Slim had to keep skipping back pages to recall. It all felt very pseudo-*Harry Potter* to Slim, except one thing.

The central character had an uncanny ability to teleport.

Much as Slim liked the concept and would have enjoyed its use to get out of a few previous tricky situations, young Claire had the unfortunate problem in that whenever she teleported, the magic it required would attract undesirables like flies to a honeypot, leaving her to battle her way out of a difficult situation each time.

Reading to the end of the tenth chapter, Slim finally closed the book and headed back for his lodgings, wondering absently whether Jennifer had somehow teleported out of existence. It would certainly explain a few things, but it would do nothing to help Elena come to terms with her grief.

After a bag of fish n' chips for lunch, Slim got to work doing the kind of drudge work he wished he could employ someone to do. Under the dubious guise of Mike Lewis, BBC researcher, he door-knocked along the rows of houses which faced the railway line, repeating a preposterous story about researching for a documentary. In particular, he told anyone who answered the door, he was on the hunt for information about a little dog which had achieved a certain level of fame during the late seventies.

Unsurprisingly, most people answered with a shrug or a suspicious frown. A couple of people, perhaps suspecting this man with fake glasses and a clipboard was sizing their house up for a burglary, told him in no uncertain terms to get lost and not come back.

But, as often happened with you sifted through enough muck, he finally came up with a little glimmer of something which showed promise.

The gum-chewing man smelled so strongly of liquor Slim had to take a step backward; not because it repulsed him but because it made him want to run for the nearest pub. He held up his clipboard like a shield and read out his list of pretend questions.

'Yeah,' the man said, nodding and frowning at the same time. 'I remember a little tyke who fits your bill. Not sure he was much of a local legend, but he was a yappy bastard, nonetheless.'

'It was your dog?'

The man shook his head. 'Oh no. I lived across the street in a council house with my mother and two brothers. Dog would show up in the garden from time to time. Kept getting through the fence, no matter how we patched it. I remember Ted—my older brother—picked it up once to throw it back over the fence and it bit his hand. Drew blood. Ted gave it a smack and chucked it back. Bloody thing still kept coming back.' He smiled as though recalling a fond childhood memory. 'We were poor, but we weren't trash, you know? Mother went over there and bollocked that old bastard who kept feeding it. Laid right into him. I remember we cheered when she came back, then we all went out for chips.'

'The owner lived across the street?'

'Don't know if he was the owner or if it were a stray he were feeding, but yeah. Old codger lived a couple of doors down. Fourteen or sixteen, one of those.'

'Do you remember the man's name?'

The man frowned. 'Nope, but it began with an L. We all called him Lichen, because he had a skin condition, made him look all scaly. Hated that old bastard, we did. Funny thing is, he probably wasn't that old. Younger than I am now, but back then as kids he might as well have been a hundred years old.'

Slim didn't like to ask for the man's age straight out, so he looked him up and down, took an educated guess and then subtracted the ten years of weathering added by the booze and cigarettes the man stank of. He was left with an age of around ten years old when Jennifer had disappeared.

'Thanks a lot,' he said, then handed the man a fake BBC business card Kim had reluctantly printed for him. 'If you think of anything else, please give me a call.'

Retreating to a small park overlooking the railway line, Slim called Kim.

'How can I help, Mr. Hardy?'

'Ah, I need you to find out anything you can about an old man who lived at number fourteen or sixteen, Stickwood Grove, Holdergate,' he said. 'I know it's not much to go on, but his surname begins with L and might have something to do with lichen,' he said.

He could almost hear Kim laughing. 'Okay, Mr. Hardy, with that limited information I'll see what I can do.'

14

STANDING IN A GOODS YARD, STARING AT A SET OF buffers, Slim felt like his own investigation had reached a similar stopping point. Waiting on return calls from a dozen or more people, most of whom he doubted would have any recollection of the strange case of Jennifer Evans, he was coming up to a beehive-kicking point. He had always found the best way to open up a case was to cause some trouble, ruffle the waters, crack open the egg of mystery and tread its contents all over the road. Unfortunately, he had always taken his inspiration from a skinful of booze, and having been dry for several weeks now he was reluctant to head back in that direction.

Across the street from Holdergate's goods yard, a pub stood on a corner next to a travel agent. Even though the booze house had once provided answers to questions he didn't know he had, on occasions it had shed light on questions of his own. In a mood to flirt with his demons, he climbed over a fence and crossed the street.

The Station Master was brighter than the kind of pub Slim had once haunted like a stumbling, lost wraith, with large skylights in a raised ceiling that revealed the cloudless blue sky. The pub was empty except for a couple of tourists leaning over a map with a pair of lattes beside them. Slim waited at the bar, and after a moment a young girl emerged through a door into a back office.

The girl was young and attractive, but even so, Slim felt disappointed. He had hoped for some grizzled old-timer steeped in local knowledge. The girl looked like a college student working a part-time job, but she smiled kindly enough and asked for his order.

The rows of liquor bottles felt like an audience at a freak show, mocking him.

'Coffee,' he muttered. 'Black. As black as it comes.'

The girl offered half a smile. 'Are there shades?'

'When you get to my age there are all sorts,' Slim said. 'If you have any from last night still in the filter, don't throw it away. Add a heaped spoonful of instant and shove it in the microwave for about thirty seconds longer than necessary.'

The girl laughed. 'I'll see what I can do,' she said.

She returned a couple of minutes later with a cup of congealed gunk that was actually pretty close to how Slim liked it. She watched him take a sip, then, as he failed to hide an approving smile, asked, 'You're a tourist?'

'I'm a trainspotter.'

She lifted an eyebrow. 'Like the Ewan MacGregor type?'

'No, the orange anorak type. Except I prefer black. It fits my personality.'

'Does it now? Shouldn't you be spotting ghost trains in that case?'

'Well, in a way I am. From 1977. I'm trying to track down a train that used to run on this line.'

'What on earth for?'

Slim took a sip of the coffee. 'I'm a nerd. And a completist.'

'And single?'

'How did you guess?'

The girl cocked her head and lifted an eyebrow. 'Could you be anything but?'

Slim shrugged. 'Believe it or not, I was married once.'

'What happened?'

'She left me for a butcher.'

The girl looked surprised. 'No jokes about meat, right?'

Slim smiled. 'Been vegetarian ever since.'

'I bet.'

'So, are you really a trainspotter or are you just winding me up?'

'I'm a private detective, but that's a secret.'

'Wow, you're really ticking off the surprise boxes now,' the girl said. 'Next thing, you'll be telling me you're a secret agent.'

'Not quite, but I was in the army. I served during the Gulf War.'

The girl lifted an eyebrow. 'Wow, that must have been interesting.'

Boots in the sand. Suddenly the coffee wasn't strong enough, but Slim swallowed down the urge to ask for something stronger and forced a smile. 'It was.'

'Good job you got him.'

'Who?'

'Saddam.'

Slim shook his head. 'We didn't. I served in the first Gulf War.'

The girl stared. 'You don't look that old.'

Slim couldn't help but laugh. 'I was straight out of

52

school. Even so, you're literally the only person who's ever said that. I got asked if I had a bus pass once, cheeky sod.'

The girl smiled. 'I tell you what. Buy me a drink and I'll tell you how I can help you track down that old train.'

Slim held her gaze, wondering if she were really flirting with him or just idling away boredom.

'Sure,' he said. 'I'll have two more coffees, please. One from the same place this dirt came from, and one nice one, for you.'

15

'LIA,' THE GIRL SAID. 'IT'S SHORT FOR AMELIA, AND YES, I prefer it.'

'Slim,' Slim said. 'Short for John. A long story, but a dull one.'

'I'll save it for the second date.'

'Then you won't want a third.'

Lia watched him, her hands cupped under her face, until he became uncomfortable and looked away. Lia was technically still on shift, but the two tourists had gone and no other customers had come in, so they had taken up a pair of comfortable window-placed armchairs which had a view of the fence surrounding the old goods yard. Through the links, a couple of old trains sat rusting away, a tumbledown shed in one corner propped up by sticks. If Slim dipped his head, he could just make out the hills rising on the other side of the station.

Lia wasn't as young as Slim had first thought, perhaps in her late twenties or early thirties. As they talked, he found himself enjoying something that he hadn't experienced in a long time: Lia's willingness to continue the conversation, as though she actually liked his company.

'So it's my friend's great-uncle who I was talking about,' she told him over their third coffee, the first two having passed during a period of pleasant if inane conversation. 'He was the station master here in Holdergate for about forty years. He's a nerd like you. He could probably recite the train times from the sixties if you wanted.'

'He's still alive?'

'In his eighties but in pretty good shape.'

'Then I'd love to talk to him.'

'I'll give my friend a call later. Are you sure you're just looking to find that old train?'

Experience had taught Slim to suspect everyone. Even though Lia wouldn't have been born when Jennifer vanished, he still felt unwilling to share too many details with a girl he had just met. And in addition, he didn't want to sour the tone of their conversation.

'I have a particular interest,' he said. 'But it's probably not interesting.'

'If you told me, I wouldn't want a second date, right?'

Slim smiled. 'That's about it.'

Lia had to do an evening shift, but her friend's great-uncle agreed to meet him based on what she said was a personal recommendation. Robert Downs was waiting in the garden at the front of his house—a twenty-minute walk from Holdergate Station—when Slim arrived at the address Lia had scribbled on the back of a beer mat.

'Slim?'

'That's me.'

Robert extended a hand. His palm felt like a soft leather glove, as though he spent all his time nowadays thumbing through books on long-forgotten trains.

'I was quite surprised when my great-niece called,' he said. 'I haven't heard a request like yours in a long time. Trainspotting is a dying hobby, you know. People get all their information from websites; no one wants to wander around in the rain.'

'I have terrible eyesight,' Slim said. 'And I prefer to be out and about.'

'Stretching out old war wounds, are you?' Robert said with a smirk. Slim, unsure if it was a serious comment or a joke, replied with a non-committal shrug.

Robert's house was on a hill north of the railway line. A view between houses across the street revealed the railway's gentle meander among fields and trees as it headed toward Manchester. The air was warm and the evening still bright, so Robert suggested they sit outside on a small terrace.

'I couldn't bear to go too far away,' Robert said, waving at the distant line. 'I worked at Holdergate Station for forty-seven years. I never felt at home anywhere else.'

A kindly old lady Robert introduced cryptically as Theresa—'my common law wife, I suppose you'd say'— brought them tea in a fetching cast iron teapot along with a plate of Digestive biscuits.

'So, it's the late seventies that you're reading up on,' Robert said, settling into a swinging cushion chair, leaving a wicker armchair for Slim. 'The local commuter trains. Easy one that. There were three run by British Rail along the Hope Valley Line. One, believe it or not, is still in service, although it had a compete refit and runs on a Scottish line now—I forget which one, but I could find out if that's the one you're after. The second got scrapped—parts probably shipped overseas. The third is in a goods yard at Manchester Piccadilly, I do believe. The goods yard there is a bit of a train graveyard. There are a few around, ostensibly in case the old locomotives are wanted for parts, but—between you and me—I've always felt there was a higher spirit who didn't like to see those old girls go. I'm sure you know what I mean.'

Slim made a mental note to ask Kim to call Manchester Piccadilly to see if he could take a look at the old train. Then, feeling that now was the moment to channel his best inner trainspotter, he smiled and said, 'Absolutely.'

'Now, if you know a specific day or time of service, I could probably track down which train it is you're after.'

Slim pulled a notebook from his pocket. 'Specifically, the eight thirty-three from Manchester Piccadilly bound for Sheffield through the winter of 1976 and early 1977.'

Almost immediately Robert's countenance darkened. He frowned at Slim, then leaned back in the chair and sighed. Its springs creaked as he swung back and forth.

'Okay, be straight with me, Mr. Hardy. It's not the train you're after. It's that woman, isn't it?'

'What woman?' Slim said, before he could stop himself, sensing even as he said it that Robert Downs had seen right through him. The guise of a trainspotter was perhaps harder to pull off than he had thought.

'Don't play me for a fool, Mr. Hardy. I spent my life working on the railways. I know a man with an interest in trains and a man after something else.'

Slim shrugged and nodded. 'Jennifer Evans,' he said. 'I

was contacted by her daughter. She asked me to look into the historical case of her mother's disappearance.'

Robert sighed. 'I thought it was too good to be true that I'd found someone with a genuine interest in those old trains.'

'I'm sorry. I was hoping that if I could track down one of the trains and take a look, I might be able to build up a picture of what happened.'

'You're a fool like all those police were, trying to find something out of nothing,' Robert said. 'The problem was that nothing happened. Nothing that anyone could figure out, at any rate. Damn event cast a cloud over my entire career.'

'You sound bitter.'

Robert shrugged. 'I suppose I am. People never looked at Holdergate Station the same after that, and for what? A girl who ran off in the snow? Probably some hippy who eloped with a lover?' He shifted on the chair, reaching out a liver-spotted hand, and picked up his cup. He finished his tea in one swallow. 'Look, I'm not really feeling up to talking about this today,' he said. 'Can you come back another time?'

Before Slim could answer, Robert stood up and went inside, slowly closing the patio doors with a deep frown on his face as though afraid he might catch Slim's foot. A lock clicked, and then curtains drew across. Slim was left sitting alone on the terrace, still with half a cup of tea to drink. He took one last sip, then stood up and headed back to his guesthouse.

'BARNARD LITCHFIELD,' KIM SAID, SOUNDING SUITABLY smug. 'He's in a nursing home on the Oldfield Estate area of Wentwood, just off Potter Street. I can email you a map if you like.'

'That would be great. Any other details?'

'He's eighty-eight years old, and has been living there since 2009. Before that he lived in a care-assisted flat outside Wentwood for roughly twenty years. I couldn't find exact dates. In 2007 he was diagnosed with dementia, so it's likely you won't get any sense from him. That's if the staff will even allow you to talk to him at all.'

'Thanks, Kim.'

'You're welcome. Glad to be of help.'

Slim walked down to the local library, where he accessed his email and printed the map Kim had sent. Oldfield Estate was on the other side of town. It had begun to rain, so Slim caught a bus.

Webster Home for the Elderly was in better shape than Slim had expected, set in attractive gardens with nice views south over the town spread out across the valley below. The building looked modern and the entrance at least was bright and welcoming. Slim showed a fake BBC identification card, told the receptionist he was researching for a documentary on local history, and asked if he might speak to some of the residents who had lived in Holdergate during the late seventies.

He was told to wait while the receptionist made some enquires. She returned with a beaming smile and said a number of residents had been assembled in the main living room. All looking forward to meeting him and sharing their memories. She told him that they didn't get much opportunity to talk about their childhood, and for many suffering from the early stages of dementia, it was beneficial to their mental health.

Slim gulped. He had hoped to speak to them one by one, but a couple of minutes later he found himself presented in front of a ring of fifteen or more wheelchairs, with a handful of others sat on regular seats. Three nurses watched from the back as Slim took a plastic chair at the front.

He hadn't rehearsed what he would ask, but had at least brought a recording device to feign his role a little better. He started by introducing himself as Mike Lewis from the BBC. With every word he felt a rush of shame for lying to these innocent people, and when a nurse, perhaps noticing how dry his throat had become from his voice, handed him a glass of water, he downed it in a single swallow.

Once the questioning began, however, he relaxed a little. The people seemed eager to talk, happily recalling tales from their younger days, many stumbling over each other to speak, with the nurses having to call for order. While Slim frantically scribbled notes to confirm his ruse as a BBC researcher, he tried to guess which of these people, if any, might be Barnard Litchfield.

Having listened to at least one tale from each of the assembled, however, Slim realised there was only one man left to speak, a guy slumped in a chair at the back, his head lolling, barely awake. His face bore scarring that could have come from an old skin condition, and the only time he moved it was to scratch absently at his arm.

Slim prepared his last question, hoping he might get a reaction.

'…I heard there was once a dog,' he said, segueing one story into another, 'that used to be seen around the station in those days. I heard it would greet the passengers. Brown or white it was, some kind of spaniel, maybe. Do any of you recall it?'

The story was utter lies apart from the dog's description. As ripples of misunderstanding filtered back, Barnard Litchfield's held lifted.

'Jedders,' he said.

One of the nurses wiped away a string of drool. He looked at another, who nodded. The first nurse began to turn Litchfield's wheelchair away.

'Jedders,' Litchfield said again. His eyes snapped open. 'Weren't no yappy thing like that, but Jedders. Met his maker under the wheels of the train.'

17

LIA SAT ACROSS FROM SLIM IN THE SOFA SEATS BY THE Old Railway's window, looking lovelier than anything Slim might have expected to willingly sit opposite him. She cupped her hands under her chin and smiled, and Slim wondered what cruel dream this was from which he might soon awake.

'I'll talk to him,' Lia said. 'I suppose the hope that you were a genuine trainspotter was too much to bear.'

'I'm not a good liar,' Slim said, thinking of the old people he had duped with lies about the BBC. He was certain he had already exhausted his karma reserves even this early in the investigation.

'I have another lead,' Slim said. 'Jedders.'

'Jedders?'

'It's a name I heard from an old man who used to live near Holdergate Station.'

'Are you sure he was in his right mind?'

'Absolutely not. He's been suffering from dementia for ten years.'

Lia laughed, then abruptly put a hand over her mouth.

'Sorry … I didn't mean … I wasn't mocking him, but are you sure you're a detective? If he's suffering from memory problems, he might not be a reliable source.'

'I'm not much of an expert on dementia, to be honest. And as someone who can barely remember last week, I'm always distrustful of memories. They have a tendency to alter over time regardless of your mental state. However, I have so little to go on that I have to follow every lead.'

'You really think you can find out what happened?'

'At this point, no, I don't. But I'm prepared to give it a little more time before I give up.'

'You're a dedicated man.'

'I think the term is "stubborn". People don't just disappear. They always go somewhere, no matter how impossible it might seem.'

'And you think this dog called Jedders might be the clue you need to break the case?'

Slim smiled. 'Searching for a stray dog from forty-odd years ago, right. You just never know. Doesn't sound very realistic, does it?'

'How about I cook you dinner, to take your mind off it all?'

Slim frowned. Lia was still watching him, her head tilted to one side as though he were a museum exhibit.

'Are you really that interested in me that you want to cook me dinner?'

'Yes. Why wouldn't I be?'

'A hundred reasons. But sure, if you really want.'

'Great. I have some things to do, but if you can come to my place about half past five, that would be great.' Lia took a little notepad from her pocket and scribbled down her address. It wasn't far; Slim recalled passing her street on the way to Robert Downs's house.

Lia excused herself, leaving Slim sitting alone by the window, wondering quite what was happening. She couldn't possibly be genuine; she was an attractive young lady and he … well, he had once been referred to as an old drunk in a duffel coat, a description that was more accurate than the speaker had realised.

Then there was the fear that some involvement between them might take his focus away from the case. With so few leads Slim was finding it hard to concentrate, but with a woman on his mind he might lose his focus altogether.

With a sigh, he stood up and went outside. A bright sun shone out of a clear blue sky, a cool breeze drifting through the streets. Slim walked up Holdergate's short high street, looking at the shop displays as he passed. He ought to get Lia some sort of present. Wine was the usual, but there was too much chance she'd expect him to drink it. In the end he went with a box of chocolates. Only as he left the shop did he realise they were labeled low calorie. With a sigh and a shrug he figured she'd have to learn about the flaws in his character sooner or later. With the chocolates in a bag under his arm, he headed back to the guesthouse to change his clothes.

He was just heading up the stairs when a door that accessed a dining room opened. For a brief moment Slim was reminded of another landlady in another guesthouse far across the country, then the woman spoke and he let the memory slide.

'Mr. Hardy? You got a letter.'

He took it and turned it over. The return address was for a Mrs. Marjorie Clifford. Slim didn't know whether he ought to be sitting down when he opened it or not. Instead, he just thanked his landlady and took it up to his room.

18

'YOU LOOK DIFFERENT,' LIA SAID, STANDING IN THE doorway as though assessing whether it was really a good idea to let Slim inside. 'And I don't just mean you've changed your shirt, brushed your hair and even had a shave. There's something else.'

Slim held up a woolly hat. 'I didn't brush my hair,' he said. Then, unsure of the protocol of first official dates, he thrust the bag of chocolates into her hand. 'I bought you these. Sorry about the type, but, well, as someone with probably twenty years on you, I know from experience that prevention is better than a cure.'

Lia frowned as she looked inside the box. 'Oh,' she said, offering a sympathetic smile. 'I appreciate you thinking of my waistline so early in our relationship. I trust you like garden salad?'

'Um, yeah.'

Lia grinned. 'Because I'm keeping the pizza for myself.'

She led Slim into a neat flat. Cramped but tidy, it had all the signs of a dutiful single daughter. Photographs on a mantle showed various younger versions of Lia with two gradually aging parents and a sister who eventually departed to form family photos of her own: first with a husband and twin daughters, to a final one of the woman by herself, and a separate, chilling photo of the man alone with the two pre-adolescent twins. Slim tried not to look too hard; he suspected the story behind it was hardly first date dinner conversation.

True to her word, Lia had rustled up a salad and a couple of other side dishes to go with a pizza steaming in its box. Slim sat down where she instructed at a table which had a night view of Holdergate through a living room window.

'Wine?'

Slim stared at the bottle, his throat suddenly dry. The temptation was heart-wrenching, as though a devil's hands had reached into his stomach and was squeezing it tight, refusing to let go until Slim relented.

'I don't … drink,' he croaked, barely able to muster the words.

'Oh, really? Don't worry … that's fine. Do you want tea instead? Orange juice?'

Lia's tone trod a fine line between confusion and mockery. Slim understood how awkward he must seem for someone she had met in a pub.

'Coffee, if you've got it. I don't sleep much either.'

He meant it as a joke, but Lia just grimaced and retreated to the kitchen, perhaps happy to be off the front line. Slim wondered if it were worth trying to explain or whether he should spin her some stupid line about being teetotal.

Lia came back with a cup of coffee so thick and black it made Slim's throat ache just to look at it. Lia grinned again. 'If you hold it upside down it stays in the cup. I'd prefer it if you trusted me though, instead of testing it over my carpet. The flat's rented.'

Slim laughed. Whether Lia had rehearsed her attempt to put him at ease, he couldn't tell, but it was appreciated.

'Thanks,' he said. Then, against his better judgement, he said, 'You drink if you want to.'

Lia perhaps had no experience with recovering alcoholics. She nodded and poured herself a glass, holding it up for a toast. As Slim stared at the sloshing liquid, he knew it would take all his willpower not to spend the rest of the evening fixated on it.

'Cheers,' he said.

He let her ask about the case, aware that he was talking too much when he should be letting her talk, but finding the wine too much of a distraction to concentrate on anything she might have to say. There were certain aspects he wanted to keep private—such as the contents of Marjorie Clifford's letter—but otherwise he found himself waxing lyrical about theoretical possibilities, some realistic, others far from it.

And his eyes were constantly checking the clock.

At ten-thirty he made his excuses to leave, citing an imaginary early appointment the next morning and an equally imaginary late night the night before. Lia looked surprised, but as he shuffled for the door she could only go along with his request.

He had hoped the fresh air would make things easier, but the smell was in his nose and wouldn't let go.

Stupid Slim, he had picked a Sunday in a quiet part of town to suffer a dramatic relapse, but a mini mart near the town centre was still open. Slim barged in past a surprised worker who was stocking crisps by the door.

'I need a drink,' Slim mumbled.

'Soft drinks over there,' the man said.

'I don't mean soft drinks.'

'Sorry, we don't sell alcohol after half past ten.'

'Look, I really need a drink. Just one of those small brandies. I'll give you twenty.'

It was nearly three times the displayed price. The man looked at the note in Slim's shaking hand and shrugged.

'Well, if you're that desperate I suppose I can ring it up in the morning,' he said.

Slim took the bottle down to the railway line, where he found a bench in a small park which overlooked the tracks. Half the bottle was already gone, and Slim feared he would need more, but the weeks of sobriety had left his tolerance low.

As he stared across the tracks at the darkness beyond, he wondered if Jennifer Evans had once sat here, on a freezing cold night, before abruptly vanishing into the air. With a shrug he realised he didn't really care.

He needed a drink.

19

He woke up in his own bed, unsure how he had got there. The door to the room was wide open, so he got up to close it, his stomach lurching at the same time. He only just made it to the sink in the corner before emptying what was left of his stomach's contents. That most of it was stinging bile suggested he'd been sick somewhere before, so with better control of his body he ventured out into the hallway and looked downstairs.

He could see the guesthouse's front door and it was shut. The carpet looked normal, with no signs of vomit, so it looked like he'd created whatever mess he had before getting back.

He returned to his room, and found a corner of his bag had blocked the door from closing. He pushed it aside, then closed and locked the door.

He sat down on the bed and ran a hand through his hair. His head was thumping, his stomach contracting, but by far the worst was the fear of what trail of destruction his drinking might have caused.

He reached for his phone—sitting beside his wallet and

keys on a dressing table, another relief—and checked for calls and messages. No outgoing calls, no outgoing messages.

He let out a long sigh. He got up again and went to the mirror above the sink in the corner, absently aware he was still fully clothed, but his face showed only the signs of a hard night of drinking. No signs of fighting or falling. His hands, too, felt fine, no telltale welts on his knuckles or aches in his wrists. Even his jeans were unscuffed, as though he'd managed to walk all the way back from the scene of meltdown without so much as falling over.

He sat down on the bed.

I can't keep living like this.

Once, hunting for the trail of destruction left by a sudden bender had been an almost daily event. He had woken up with bruises a dozen times, wondering who had hit him, who he had hit. Where he had lost his stuff. Who he had called up in the middle of the night, blathering at like an idiot, or worse, ranting, berating. Who had now blacklisted his number. Who would never again let him inside their home.

I can't keep living like this.

He picked up his phone and called Lia.

'Oh. Slim. Hi.'

'I'm sorry about yesterday,' he croaked.

'Well, you did leave rather abruptly.'

'Not just that. Everything. Can I meet you? Please. It's important.'

'Well … I don't work until twelve, so we could meet somewhere for breakfast if you like.'

'Thanks.'

~

His stomach still felt like a broken washing machine, but his headache had been tempered by a couple of ibuprofen. He arrived half an hour early and was on his third coffee when Lia arrived just before ten.

She came to the table but stayed standing until he asked her to sit. She had dressed down, but her hair was brushed and she wore a little makeup. The look on her face was one of distress. Until she spoke, Slim thought it was horror at his own appearance, one reason he didn't own a mirror and avoided them where possible.

'So,' she said, unable to meet his eyes. 'This is where you tell me you're married, right? I mean, I know you said you were single, but men tend to delude themselves—'

Slim couldn't help but laugh. Despite the seriousness in her eyes he doubted there was anything she could have said that he would have found more ridiculous.

'No, I'm not married, and aside from a couple of flings that didn't turn out well, I've been single most of the last twenty years.'

'So what's this sudden emergency meeting about then? I mean, that's how it feels. I guess you're too old to break up with me by phone like younger men might.'

'I didn't even realise we were going out.'

'Well, I mean, not yet, but I like you, you know.'

'And I like you too. I wasn't expecting to meet someone I liked while investigating forty-year-old trains.'

'Then what's the problem?'

Slim brought it down like a hammer blow. 'I'm an alcoholic.' At Lia's look of surprise, he added, 'Recovering. Well, I was.'

Lia sighed. 'The wine.'

'I thought I could handle it. In the bottle I might have, but seeing it in the glass, the smell … the way it sloshed as

71

you drank it … even the sound it made as you swallowed … I tried, I really did.'

'I'm sorry.'

'No. I should have said. I just … I thought I could handle it. I'm afraid I went into panic mode. You must have thought I was off my head as it was.'

Lia shrugged. 'Well, you did seem a little off after we sat down for dinner.'

Slim reached across the table and put a hand over Lia's. It felt strange to touch a woman and not have her flinch away. He looked up into her eyes and saw the concern there.

'I'm a pretty messed up person,' he said. 'To be honest, there have been times when I'm not sure how I get through the days. But I'm also not a project case. I like you. I think you're a fascinating person, not to mention beautiful. I'll warn you now that you'd be better off walking away from me. It's unlikely I can make you happy for long, no matter how hard I try.' He forced a smile. 'But if you don't, I won't mind.'

Lia held his gaze for a few seconds, then gently removed his hand and stood up.

'I need to think about this,' she said.

'That's fine. That's probably the best thing.'

Lia gave him a half smile and retreated back through the tables to the door. She went out and gave him a brief wave through the window before hurrying away across the street.

Slim watched her go. When she was out of sight, he sighed, ordered another coffee and pulled Marjorie Clifford's letter out of his bag.

20

Dear Mr. Hardy,

Thank you for your letter. My apologies in keeping you waiting for so long for a response, but I have arthritis in my hands and find it hard to hold a pen for a long period of time.

Then there's the subject matter. I'm afraid that your correspondence invoked memories I've not had in years. Don't misunderstand me; they weren't all bad. Jennifer was my best friend on the staff during my junior years at M.R.I. and I have fond memories of her. However, her sudden disappearance stunned me like it did many others, and in many ways it changed the whole course of my life. I'm not sure how much research you've done on my background, but I left nursing the following year and moved down to Cornwall. It wasn't the job so much as Manchester and the spectre of Jennifer. I couldn't handle crowds any longer because I found myself forever looking for her among them, so I moved to the remotest place I could find. I got work in a café, but even that was hard, and it was years before I could hear the bell over the door without looking up in expectation of somehow seeing her face.

There have been days when I wished they'd found her, whatever horror story it might have revealed. Better that than to forever wonder.

But I'm afraid I digress. You asked specifically if there was anything I might know about her final movements, about what might have happened to her.

The last time I saw her was in the staff locker room at around eight p.m. Some days we shared the same shift, but that week she was on days while I was doing nights, so her shift had just finished while mine was about to begin. I saw her pack up her bag as usual and store her uniform in her locker. Her next shift was due to start at ten the following morning.

There was nothing untoward about her behaviour. Her state of mind, however, was a different matter. We worked together at that time in the Coronary Care Unit, but I know she had been sneaking off duty regularly over the last few weeks to visit a patient on the oncology ward, who I believe had terminal cancer of some kind. His name was Jim Randall. I remember her saying something about wishing she could turn the clock back. No, a little different: "I wish I could have my time over again." That was it, I'm sure. I know it was a long time ago, but I remember it clearly because it was such a negative thing for Jennifer to say. She was always so positive, so forward-thinking. She was a very God-fearing person, never forgetting her prayers, and she believed in positive thinking, that you could almost will something to turn out right. Working on the CCU, that was important, when many of the patients had come there specifically to find comfort in their last days. Recoveries were few and far between, but Jennifer

74

believed in everyone, that with a little willpower and faith they might achieve some miracle of remission. With Jennifer, life was never about yesterday, it was always about tomorrow. That was the kind of person she was, so I remember dwelling on those words during my shift that night.

Of course early that next morning I found out about Jennifer's disappearance. I couldn't help but think about what she had said. And I wondered if it had had anything to do with Jim Randall. Jim Randall was a patient on the oncology ward up the corridor from our own. Jennifer had told me about visiting him, helping him to find God in his suffering. I went to see him, to ask if she had said anything untoward before going home that evening, but was told he had died during the afternoon on the previous day.

If she had been aware of his death, it would have explained Jennifer's mood somewhat, although not her words, as I knew nothing of the nature of their relationship. It wasn't uncommon for us nurses to take particular note of a patient even if they were on another ward, especially if we had had some contact with them on their admittance. However, I always felt that her disappearance might be connected to Jim's death. I don't like to speculate, but I did tell the police of my suspicions. Unfortunately I believe nothing came of it. And there, I'm afraid, Mr. Hardy, is the end of what I have to say. I pray that something of this might prove useful. I'm not in the best of health these days, and I hope sadly that you will have no more need of me. Although, saying that, if you ever do find out what became of Jennifer, I'd very much like to know.

Yours faithfully,

Marjorie Clifford

21

'NOTHING,' CHARLES BOSWORTH SAID, LEANING ACROSS the table. 'We checked him out. He was a homeless drifter with no background, admitted after collapsing on a Manchester street. He had advanced lung cancer and died a couple of weeks after admittance. We couldn't find any background information for him, but to be honest, we didn't look that hard. The man was dead; he could hardly be a suspect.'

Slim lifted a hand, but Bosworth cut him off.

'Before you say anything, yes, we did consider that they might have had some kind of a relationship, and that his death may have had an effect on her. It was as big a lead as we had. I actually kept the information from her family, but all known local suicide spots—plus a few farther afield —were checked in the days after her disappearance. We found nothing. We had to let it go.'

'Did you interview the nurses on the oncology ward?'

Bosworth threw up his hands. 'We interviewed the staff on duty that day, but the full roster … no. We just didn't have the resources in those days, and Jennifer's disappearance was low priority. Without a body there was no murder inquiry and our investigations threw up few suspicious leads. I worked on the case in my own time for a while, but in the end it got filed.'

'It's a lead,' Slim said. 'What if she had known him?'

'No one we spoke to had any knowledge of a nurse from another ward coming to visit him. We assumed Marjorie Clifford's claim was a little exaggerated. And in any case, Jim Randall was dead. He could hardly have come back to life and snatched her, could he? Besides, she made that call to her daughter. What might have made her suddenly change her mind?'

Slim shrugged. 'I have no idea.' He looked up. 'I have another lead. Jedders. I believe it was the name of a dog which lived near Holdergate Station.'

'Jedders? What kind of a name for a dog is that?'

'I thought maybe it was Jed but people called it Jedders as a nickname.'

Bosworth whistled as he shook his head. 'And the significance of this dog is what?'

'It could have caused the teeth marks on the bag, not a wild animal like you thought. If I can ascertain who owned the dog or what time it might have been roaming about outside, it could give a better indication of what time Jennifer lost her bag, not to mention that she could have been in close proximity of the dog's owner.'

Bosworth nodded. 'Slim, you're certainly bringing a level of energy to this that I can no longer muster. I still think there's nothing to it, but out of interest, where did you hear the name?'

'A man called Barnard Litchfield. Unfortunately, he's eighty-eight and suffering from dementia.'

'So it could have been just nonsense.'

'Yes. For all I know, it was the plot of the television show he'd watched the night before I spoke to him, but I won't dismiss it immediately.'

Bosworth stared at him. 'For what it's worth, I'm cheering for you. Don't give up.'

Slim didn't want to tell Bosworth that at this exact moment, it was only the case keeping him out of the nearest pub. Instead, he just nodded. I'll follow it until I run out of leads, I suppose.'

He left Bosworth's house and went to another meeting with Elena. He had arranged to meet her in a park near Holdergate Station, so picked up coffee for them both at a local café along the way.

When he arrived, Elena looked up, her eyebrows immediately rising in expectation, shifting on the bench as though she meant to leap to her feet. He hated the way she always looked so hopeful, but at least today he had some leads to discuss.

'I wondered if I might ask you a little about your grandparents on your mother's side,' he said. 'It could be significant. This might be hard to talk about, but I wondered if they had any skeletons in the closet.'

At Elena's look of distress, Slim gave her a reassuring pat on the arm. 'Just to be clear, I'm not accusing them of anything. It's just that I'm trying to connect people who might have been involved.'

Elena shrugged. 'They were as strait-laced as a couple could be. Married nearly sixty years, devoted in that nonchalant way where old couples consider each other part of the furniture. Three kids, my mother was the middle one, between two boys. Both my uncles were married and had simple lives. The older one died a few years ago. The younger one is still alive but in a care home

78

on the south coast. Both were living in London at the time of my mother's disappearance. They both came back to help with the search.'

'Can you find me pictures? The older the better.'

'Sure. I have boxes of them. What's this about, Mr. Hardy?'

'I'm not sure. Just a line of enquiry, one of many.'

'I'm glad you're finding some. The police drew a blank.'

'Mine are tentative at best. Can I ask you if you've ever heard the word "Jedders"?'

Elena shrugged. 'Doesn't ring any bells. What does it mean?'

'That's what I'm trying to find out.'

'I can't say that I have. It's that odd that I might remember it.'

'Well, if something comes to mind, don't hesitate to contact me.'

Elena nodded. 'I thank you, Mr. Hardy.'

'What for?'

'For trying.'

Slim let her shake his hand then bid her goodbye. He wondered as he walked away whether he should have asked about Jim Randall. Maybe Elena knew the name, but in the meantime he wanted to keep Randall close to his chest, unveiling his cards one at a time to avoid them influencing each other.

He walked back toward the high street, but as soon as he was out of sight he doubled back and headed for the station.

There, he caught a train to Manchester.

22

JUST AFTER QUARTER TO MIDDAY, HE CLIMBED DOWN from a small but crowded train and looked around. It had been a while since he'd last willingly gone to a major city and he found himself feeling a little overwhelmed. He had always preferred small towns because it was easier to avoid the vices that always seemed to find him. Here, though, he was looking for just that: the seedier side, the underbelly. Whether the city would provide was another matter. A couple of hours on the internet at Holdergate Library had provided him with a list of the areas in modern Manchester considered most downtrodden by public opinion. From outside the station he caught a hopper bus into the city centre, walked to Piccadilly Bus Station and caught a commuter bus up to Church Street.

He'd been kidnapped, beaten up, and stabbed, and that had been since he'd left the Armed Forces. He felt less fear walking through the tougher streets than he generally did walking through woods, almost as though it were the familiarity of a situation that soothed him. Having not so long ago been among the down and outs, he also felt something like kinship with the people living in Britain's social cracks. It wasn't long before he started to see the kind of people he was looking for.

A group of obvious drug users sauntered up the street in his direction. One absently requested change as they passed, but the others ignored him, his face perhaps marking him as one of them.

'Hey!' he called, turning around.

'What do you want?' said the nearest, turning around and spreading his hands as though spoiling for a fight.

'I'm looking for information,' Slim said. 'I'm trying to track someone down.'

'Who the hell are you?'

'I'm a nobody looking for another nobody. Think you can help me?'

He reached into his pocket and pulled out a crumpled pile of banknotes and a handful of creased business cards which only had his name and phone number. He tossed a couple of tenners on the ground and watched the nearest man scramble to scoop them up.

'I've got more if you can find me who I need,' Slim said. 'How does a grand sound?'

'And what do you want in return?'

'I'm looking for a dead man, information on him. A man called Jim Randall. He was on the street back in the seventies, maybe even the sixties. He died in 1977. I want you to find me someone old enough that they might have known that man. Someone who might have grown up on the streets during that time.'

'You'll be lucky.'

'So will you be if you find someone.'

'We'll be in touch,' the man said, grinning. Slim watched him turn and swagger away up the street, his companions close behind, bickering over the money the first man clutched in his hand. As they reached a corner, the first man glanced back over his shoulder and started laughing, as though sure he had played Slim for a mug.

When they had disappeared from sight, Slim shrugged and carried on his way. It was likely he would never see the men nor hear from them again, but it was a seed planted, and if he planted enough, maybe a tree would grow.

He headed on, looking for the next person who fit his criteria, a thousand pounds in crumpled used notes padding out his pocket.

He stopped in mid-afternoon for an early dinner, before heading out again as darkness descended over the city. After dark he expected to find his most likely candidates. Tracking down the homeless wasn't hard, it was finding those with a connection to a man dead more than forty years that was tough. Slim's best hope was to encounter someone who had sorted their life out, moved on from a troubled past.

With his money running out, he began making the rounds of homeless shelters, asking for information. A couple of people laughed and shrugged off his request as fanciful. One older volunteer took him into an office room, offered him coffee then promised to ask around.

It was as much as he could hope for. No one stayed on the streets for forty years. You either got off the street or you died there. Exhausted, Slim caught the last train back to Holdergate and barely reached his guesthouse on his feet. As he climbed into bed, though, he felt more grateful for the comfort of soft clean sheets than he had done in a long time.

23

'A MAN CAME BY YESTERDAY, ASKING FOR YOU,' THE guesthouse owner, Wendy, told Slim over breakfast. 'He gave me a business card to pass on. If you can hang on a moment, I'll just go and hunt out where I put it.'

Slim was running through a list of people who might know how to find him, everyone from Robert Downs to an ex-boyfriend of Lia's who might have taken umbrage at his treatment of her. When he looked at the name printed on the card Wendy was holding out, he was so stunned he must have shown surprise, because Wendy said, 'Not who you were expecting, I'll suppose?'

Slim smiled as he took the card. 'Not really,' he said. 'Thanks for keeping it.'

Tobin P. Firth. Beneath the name was just a mobile number. On the other side, in swirling letters: *Children's author.*

'I'm afraid I didn't have anything he'd written so I had him sign a *Harry Potter*,' Wendy swooned. 'He seemed to see the funny side. Friend of yours?'

'I'm not sure yet,' Slim said. 'We've never met.'

Wendy didn't seem to find this odd, just shrugged and excused herself to go and clean up the dishes. Slim took the card and walked down the road to the small park at the end before he took it out again to call the number.

The call was answered on the second ring. 'Slim Hardy, is that you?' came a soft, almost childlike voice, and Slim could almost imagine he was talking to that same boy who had been the last to see Jennifer Evans alive.

'It's me,' Slim said. 'I'm honored that you got in touch. It was a surprise to hear you came to my guesthouse.'

'When I got your message—well, perhaps it would be better if we talked in person. Where are you now?'

'In the park at the end of the street from where I'm staying.'

'I took a room across the street from you,' came the reply. 'I'll be there in fifteen minutes.'

Slim had to remind himself that Tobin P. Firth was older than he. Boyish, with the look of years of soft living about him, Tobin was clean shaven, plump and wide-eyed. A little shorter than Slim, in a leather jacket that had probably cost more than Slim's last car, he looked like an enthusiastic school kid about to embark on an adventure.

'Call me Toby,' he said. 'Tobin's just a pen name. It's not even mine. And the P stands for "pen", just to remind me.'

'Sure, Toby,' Slim said. 'Slim is kind of a pen name of my own. Just no pens involved.'

'I won't ask,' Toby said.

'Don't. It's not an interesting story.'

It was a warm spring day with not a cloud in the sky. In the park's corner, a light breeze was buffeting the long grass left by the turning circle of a wheeled mower. Slim sat across from Toby on a wooden bench with a view between two lines of houses of the high moors rising in the distance.

'I tried to read one of your books,' Slim said. 'I'm afraid I'm not much of a reader. I try from time to time but I rarely get more than a few chapters in before giving up.'

Toby laughed. 'You don't look like the kind of person who'd be into young adult fantasy,' he said. 'More like gritty crime, I'd imagine.'

Slim nodded. 'And I live it enough to not need to read it.'

Toby nodded, mumbling something illegible under his breath, and then let out a long sigh. 'Let's just cut to it, Slim. You want to know what I saw. It doesn't matter why on Earth of everything you could have done, you've chosen to dig up this mystery. You want to know what I saw, and I want to tell you.'

'I'm glad.'

Toby squeezed his eyes shut and rubbed the bridge of his nose. 'Goddamn, if that night didn't alter the entire course of my life. And all I've ever wanted was to tell it how I remember.'

'Tell me. It might mean nothing, or it might mean everything. What did you see that night, and what did Jennifer see?'

Toby whistled. 'I never told the police, because I didn't want to get my back whipped by my dad thinking I was a liar. I mean, I was a kid but I wasn't stupid. I knew it couldn't be what I thought, but that's what I saw. And I knew it was serious. It was the police, not just some kids at school.'

'What did you see?'

Toby looked at Slim, fixing him with a firm stare. 'I saw a man vanish into thin air.'

24

THERE WAS AN OLDE-WORLDE PUB CALLED THE Ironmonger's Arms on the corner of the street opposite the church, eaves that might have been fake overhanging where a man stood talking on his mobile phone and sucking on a vape. Inside, Slim ordered a pint of Stella for Toby and a pint of alcohol-free for himself, praying he could hold himself together. He excused himself to take a bathroom break where he splashed water on his face, and when he came back, Toby had already drunk half his beer and bought in two more. Slim stared at the two full drinks, unable to be sure which was the first one he had bought, and fearing what Toby, unaware of Slim's condition, might have ordered. In the end, he picked up the nearest, taking a small sip, finding it had that coppery tingle of alcohol. He moved his hands away.

'Control,' he whispered.

'I wasn't about to tell the police because I knew they wouldn't believe me,' Toby was saying. 'So I said nothing about it at all. I didn't want them to think I was lying, and like I say, my dad was a hard bastard if I misbehaved.'

From the way Toby took a long drink after his explanation, his eyes gazing off into space, Slim felt sure only half the story was being told.

'You were six years old,' Slim said. 'I fell off my bike and split my elbow around the age of five, but that's practically my only memory of the first few years of my life. How can you be sure of what you saw, so long after?'

'I don't need to be sure,' Toby said, slugging back another quarter of a pint and then wiping his mouth on his sleeve as though he were still six years old. 'I have proof. The photograph.'

'I've seen it,' Slim said. 'All it shows is the footprints in the snow. There's no proof Jennifer saw anything.'

Toby shrugged and took another swig of beer, making Slim, trying to hold himself together by taking small sips of his pint, wonder who had the drinking problem.

'Yeah, that's the one I gave to the police,' Toby said, looking up to meet Slim's eyes. 'The one of the footprints in the snow. I was happy enough to hand that one over.' He took a long sigh that seemed to involve his entire upper body, and Slim wondered if he was about to cry. 'But that wasn't the only one. There's another.'

Slim was sure the photograph would look clearer if he was sober, but it was too late for that. He had done better than expected, consuming at his best estimate less than half that of his drinking partner, but he still found himself staring at the photograph through a drunken haze, aware that nearby, bestselling children's author Tobin P. Fifth was sobbing into his sixth or seventh beer.

'I'm not afraid anymore,' Toby said, wiping his eyes.

'That bastard can't hurt me. He can't call me a liar, call me useless, a fag, a sissy, because I'm right. I was right all along. Wasn't I? Wasn't I, Slim?'

Slim tried to say something about helping Toby find a therapist, but he wasn't sure what words actually came out. All he could do was stare at the picture in his hands.

'It's not the original,' Toby said, wiping his eyes. 'I keep that locked away. This is an enlarged version. You can keep it.'

'It's blurry. Is that the copy or my eyes?'

'The original is the same. I had a few copies done at a photo shop a few years back, in case I ever lost the original. It's as good as it could be.'

'Well, thanks.'

Toby stabbed a finger at the picture, almost hard enough to crease it. 'See? I wasn't lying. I took these pictures back to back, less than thirty seconds apart. There's Jennifer. There's her tracks. But the man ... no tracks.'

The man. The first picture, taken moments before the second, showed Jennifer turning on her heels, arms flailing out to her sides as though she were about to do a pirouette. Where her feet scuffed the snow was clearly visible.

And there at the top of the picture, arms folded as he stood in the shadows beneath a line of trees that overhung the fence bordering Holdergate Park, stood a man. Visible in the first picture, gone in the second. No sign of tracks, nothing.

Slim looked up. 'And you saw this? You saw him vanish?'

'I was taking a picture of the street,' Toby said. 'She wandered into shot just as I was lining it up. I guess she looks a little blurred because of the length of the exposure, plus the light was poor. She was moving, you see? That's why. After she ran off, I liked the way her footprints had left a trail, so I took another. Only then did I think about what had happened, so I looked around for her, but assumed she had gone back to the train. I didn't really look at the pictures until we were back on board a couple of hours later, after they had cleared the line. Someone was serving up soup in the waiting room, so my mother called me in.'

'You didn't see Jennifer?'

Toby shook his head. 'No. I assumed she'd gone to sit back on the train.'

'But did you see this man? Out there on the street?'

Toby looked up. 'He was standing right there, just watching the parking area at the front of the station as though he was waiting for someone but didn't want them to see him first. Yeah, I saw him. I looked down to take the picture. I was actually trying to cut him out, but I'd never used a camera before and it was a Polaroid, so you had a wait before you knew what you'd taken. Then out comes Jennifer. Starts walking across the road, looks up, sees this guy, turns on her heel and bolts. The guy didn't move, just stood there. I lift the camera, take another shot. I'm looking through the lens, he's there. Look up … he's gone. Vanished. I went outside to take a look, but there was no sign of him, just Jennifer's tracks in the snow.'

Slim didn't know what to make of Toby's explanation, but he suspected by the speed Toby was throwing back drinks that his memory had become somewhat distorted over the last forty-two years.

'What did you make of it all at the time?'

'I was a kid. Yeah, it was spooky, but all just a big adventure. Even more so when I saw those pictures, and it wasn't until a long time after that I really understood what was going on.' He looked down. 'I mean, until I got home, and then … well.'

Slim frowned. He wasn't sure he wanted to know what had happened later, but Toby had left the situation dangling, and Slim felt it polite to ask.

'I … I knew I shouldn't have gone out in the snow,' Toby said, breaking out into sobbing again. 'I had new shoes. I wasn't to get them mucky. And the camera … it was a present. I wasn't looking after it well enough.' The look of utter horror in Toby's eyes made Slim wish he'd never got in contact. 'He made me sorry,' Toby whimpered. 'He made me sure I'd never do it again.'

Other customers had begun to notice them. Slim, usually the drunkest in any drinking party, muttered an apology in the direction of the bar, and then helped Toby outside into the sunshine. They walked down the street, and Slim was happy he could feign sobriety long enough to buy a bottle of brandy from a corner shop. They went over to Holdergate Park and found a bench in a quiet corner where they shared the bottle. Slim, feeling miserable and just wanting to drink alone and in peace, found himself consoling an increasingly rambling Toby as the writer descended into a chaos of suppressed memories, few of which were clear, and even fewer of which made much sense. By the time Slim had finally directed Toby home, he was left wondering if he could believe a single word the writer had told him, or whether he was simply part of the plot for a new book Toby had decided to brainstorm on a whim.

It was dark when Slim finally stumbled back to his lodgings. He crawled up the stairs, slipped into his room and collapsed on the bed, aware that he was beginning to lose control once more, something he couldn't afford to do if he wanted to keep a handle on the case.

As he remembered something Toby had told him just before they parted, he wondered if perhaps what he had thought would be a clean and simple missing persons case was turning out to be an investigation darker than his sanity could handle.

Toby, bloodshot eyes filled with tears: 'I still have the scar behind my ear where he broke the camera over my head. Mother had already gone into the house. He told her I slipped in the snow.'

25

THE HANGOVER WAS ALL-CONSUMING. SLIM VOMITED into the little sink, cleaned it up as best he could, then drank as much water as he could handle, vomited that, and then repeated the process, hoping to clean out his guts a little. He showered and dressed, making himself as presentable as possible, before stumbling downstairs for the guesthouse's complimentary breakfast.

Feeling a little better with some greasy fry-up in his stomach, he went to the park at the end of the street and called Kay Skelton, a former army friend who now worked in forensics.

'Slim, is that you? It's been a while. How are you doing?'

Slim smiled, always happy to hear Kay's voice. 'I'm surviving,' he said. 'Working a new case in the Peak District. I wanted to pick your brains about photography. I'm wondering about exposures and lighting. How they could make a person appear in one picture, then gone in the next.'

'Slim, I'm a forensic linguist; this is hardly my specialist field. As always, I'll ask around, see if I can unearth someone who might know. What exactly are you looking for?'

'I'm chasing a ghost.'

Kay laughed. 'Good luck.'

Slim hung up. As he did so, he noticed a voicemail message box. Opening it, he found a message from Toby, apologising for the previous night and wanting to meet again later, when he was feeling better.

Slim didn't call back. Instead, he walked down to the station and caught the next train that stopped at Wentwood. There, he walked to the library—a larger one than Holdergate's—and spent some time going through old newspapers again.

By lunchtime, the pull of the nearest pub was insidious, so he took the first road heading out of the town and walked uphill until his feet hurt and his stomach ached. He found a small lookout point and lay down on the grass, trying to visualise the scene as it must have been on the night of January 15th, 1977. Jennifer, moments after hanging up a call to tell her daughter she would be home soon, walking out into the snow. Seeing something that shocked her—it had to be the man, but Slim was keeping every option open—then turning in her tracks and fleeing, never to be seen again.

The biggest mystery was who she had seen that night, the supposedly vanishing man photographed by Toby Firth. But it had to go deeper than that. As Slim concentrated, he started to see a deeper scenario, one in which a woman was faced with a tough walk through unexpected snow heavy enough to delay a train. Her daughter was at home, but at twelve—particularly in those days when children grew up quicker than they did now—

94

Elena would have been capable of looking after herself, and even had she not, surely her father would have been home? Why would Jennifer have foregone the offer of soup and a warm station waiting room for a traipse of an hour or more through snow that along the old bridleway might have drifted to knee deep in places?

Three reasons, as far as Slim could see. The first two seemed unlikely: that she had seen someone who scared her outside or she had gone to meet someone.

But what about the third? That she had a reason to get home so great that she literally couldn't wait.

Slim sat up and opened his eyes. Blinking in the sunlight, suddenly bright as the sun emerged from behind a cloud, he pulled out his phone and called Elena.

26

'MR. HARDY, ARE YOU INSINUATING THAT THERE MIGHT have been something amiss about my family?'

Slim frowned into his coffee, unable to meet Elena's eyes. 'I'm not insinuating anything,' he said. 'I'm just trying to look at the case from every possible angle.'

'Don't beat about the bush. You think that my mother might have been in a rush to get home that night because of something my father might do to me.'

To deny it would be a lie. Faced by the anger in Elena's eyes, Slim could only shrug.

'It crossed my mind,' he admitted. 'Figuring out your mother's motivation for leaving the warmth and comfort of that station is paramount to finding out what happened to her. However, it's worth remembering that it might not be something that actually happened. It might have just been something your mother thought was going to happen.'

Elena wiped a tear out of her eye. 'I had high hopes for this investigation,' she said. 'But I'm not sure how much longer I can keep paying you. You've found nothing concrete whatsoever and as a result you're trying to soil my memories of my parents by insinuating heinous things.'

Slim declined to point out that when you dug for dirt that was often what you found. It wouldn't help and would only hinder Elena's progress through the denial stage he hoped would soon pass. He needed some actual information.

'I know this is hard to talk about, but is there anything from the last few weeks before your mother's disappearance that seemed out of the ordinary? Anything at all—behaviour that seemed odd, unfamiliar phone callers, meetings with people you'd never seen before, secrecy of any kind … anything like that could be a clue.'

Elena frowned for a long time. Finally she shook her head.

'No, nothing. Not that I remember.'

'It might seem insignificant.'

'It was a long time ago.'

Slim, who often struggled to remember the events of the previous day, could sympathise. 'Just let me know if anything comes back.'

'Of course.' Elena took a sip of tea, leaving an awkward silence to develop. Finally she said, 'So, do you have any leads at all?'

Slim grimaced. 'More than when we started, but I'll be honest with you, it's proving hard to get much headway. I'm confident that some of the leads I've uncovered will give us something to go on, however. I was expecting this case to be easy to crack, and it's certainly not proving to be.'

Elena mulled this over her tea. Slim was reluctant to offer her much hope when he was fearful that all he might uncover would be more dirt.

After a few minutes more of covering ground they had already been over, Slim made his excuses then took the train up to Wentwood, where he met Mark Buckle in a sandwich bar not far from the station.

'Thanks for meeting me again,' Slim said, gesturing to the menu. 'I'll get this.'

Buckle laughed. 'I'm officially out on business,' he said. 'So it's all good. Going on the expense account.' After they had both ordered, Buckle choosing a vegetarian roll and Slim a meatball sandwich with chili sauce he hoped would burn the relapse out of his stomach, Buckle added, 'So, how's your investigation coming?'

Slim grimaced. 'Slowly. I wanted to ask you more about the Evans family, in particular the father. I remember what you said about how hard he worked during the search, but I'm trying to establish a reason why Jennifer might have felt a special need to get home that night, despite the blizzard. Something … inappropriate.'

Buckle nodded. 'You think the father might have been messing around with the daughter?'

'It crossed my mind.'

'And let me guess, when you put it to Elena, it didn't go down well.'

Slim sighed. 'Not at all.'

'You know, that kind of questioning is likely to cause more damage than it's worth,' Buckle said. 'This is a buried case. If, for example, something was going on, then it's been long-suppressed. If you're going to drag it up again, you'd sure as hell better hope you find Jennifer. Otherwise you could do more harm than good.'

Slim nodded. Buckle had put into words exactly how he thought. 'It was never my intention when I took this case to destroy anyone's life,' he said. 'If anything, I took it because I hoped, after a couple of tough cases, it might prove to be nothing more than a gentle distraction for a few weeks. Unfortunately, it isn't turning out that way. And sometimes, if you want to overturn the stones other people have missed, you have to ask the questions no one else is prepared to ask.'

Buckle cocked his head. 'That may be true, but one thing that's safe to assume is that Jennifer isn't coming back, and in the intervening years her family repaired itself in the best way it could. Elena's life might not be as she'd like it, but it's probably better as it is than if you dig up something about her mother having an affair, or her father being a child molester.'

'My intention is only to find out what happened to Jennifer. I didn't expect it to lead into the dark places it's starting to go.'

'All crimes are connected to that dark place,' Buckle said. 'It's the reason I went to work for the *Chronicle*'s Rural Affairs section. I preferred writing about farming practices than mangled bodies.'

'Was there nothing you suspected at the time?'

'Of course there was. I wondered the same thing as you, but there was no evidence for it and I worked for a broadsheet, not a scummy tabloid.'

'Her father seemed outside suspicion?'

'On a social scale, he was a nobody. A simple family man. The kind of person who your eyes would slide over in a crowd. He worked an office job, came home, did the usual dad things of those days: watch TV or occasionally saunter down the local pub. I interviewed a few people who knew the family. The overwhelming response was that they were as normal and boring as a family could come, with nothing particular about them to set them apart. Just, you know, regular people.'

'The normal families usually have the most to hide,' Slim said. 'You said he was an office worker. What company?'

'He worked in the claims department of a commercial car insurance company called Astak National. About as boring as you could get.'

'Commercial claims?'

'They specialised in discount insurance for fleets of vehicles, for example transportation companies, building contractors. That kind of thing. Companies these days are more catch-all than they used to be. As far as I'm aware, though, Astak National was bought out by a larger company sometime in the mid-eighties.'

Slim thanked Buckle for his time and headed back to Holdergate, feeling a creeping sense of disillusionment about the investigation and where—if anywhere—it was leading.

As he was exiting the station, he saw Lia clearing a table through the window of the Station Master. Unsure what he was thinking, he found himself going in through the door.

'Hello, stranger,' Lia said, offering more of a smile than Slim felt he deserved. 'I wondered if you mightn't have given up.'

'I'm too stupid to give up,' Slim said. 'Can I buy you dinner?'

Lia laughed. 'No. However, you can buy yourself dinner and sit and talk to me while I finish my shift. Then, when I get off at nine you can escort me past the Tesco Metro so I can buy a sandwich, then come and drink coffee in my kitchen while I eat it. If I'm in a good mood

I'll let you sit with me while I watch News at Ten, then I'll kick you out so I can get a decent sleep without worrying about you sneaking off to drink my mouthwash in the middle of the night. How does that sound?'

'It's a date,' Slim said.

27

AGAINST WHAT SHE SAID WAS HER BETTER JUDGEMENT, Lia let him stay overnight. However, concerned with overstaying his welcome, Slim told Lia he had early appointments and made his excuses to leave before it was even fully light outside, arranging to meet her later for lunch.

Holdergate was just waking up as he walked back to his guesthouse, hoping Wendy would already have gotten up and unlocked the front door. The streets, admirably clean, had an old-fashioned feel when cars were absent, and Slim found himself recalling his childhood, the meat of it during the mid-eighties when the music was as blandly electric as the fashion was gaudy. He remembered walking up to the corner shop in a dark purple shell-suit to buy football cards and chocolate bars in the carefree days before he had started to drink, before the last innocence was shaken out of him by the army and a pair of boots in the sand, before his fading dreams of a normal life were stamped out by a butcher named Stiles, a knife, and a crumpled abortion letter in a rubbish bin. He sometimes thought it would be more of a surprise if he didn't drink.

With a few kind words and an unprecedented level of tolerance, Lia had made him feel normal and valuable in a way no one had in twenty years. The fragile scaffolding of his returning happiness would inevitably come crashing down, but the way Lia had made him feel gave him reason alone to extend the case.

If only he could get a break, everything would be perfect.

He was back at the guesthouse in time for breakfast and had just finished when his Nokia rang. It was Toby, wanting to meet. Twenty minutes later, Slim was waiting in the park where they had first met when Toby arrived.

'I'm sorry again about the other night,' Toby said. 'I guess I still have some issues. A bit of booze tends to bring it out.'

Slim considered mentioning that there hadn't been much booze left by the time Toby was done, but decided it wouldn't help. Instead he just said, 'It was interesting to hear things from your perspective.'

'So, do you think you might be able to find Jennifer?'

Slim shrugged. 'At the moment I have a list of names and numbers as long as my arm with no idea who might be worth calling first.'

'I want to help,' Toby said.

'Help?'

'To find her.'

'I'm not sure—' Slim began, but Toby held up a hand.

'On the surface it might look like I have everything,' he said. 'Without mincing my words, I'm loaded. I'm only halfway through a ten-book deal and each release sells more than the last. I have a nice house in London, a beautiful wife, two good kids in a private school. I'm made, wouldn't you think?'

'On the surface,' Slim said, echoing Toby's words, only too aware that demons could hide beneath any skin.

'There's a knot inside me that's growing tighter as the years pass. I see buses go past and I think about how it would feel to step out at exactly the wrong time. I stop my car on bridges and get out, gazing down at the water for longer than I feel safe. I don't trust myself, Slim. And it's all because of that knot inside that got tied on the night Jennifer went missing.'

'Toby—'

'Look, I'll be in Holdergate for the next week. I'm doubling it as time to research my next book. If there's any way at all I can help, I'm here. Just ask.'

Slim nodded. 'Sure. I'd certainly like to go over again what you saw. Just to make it clear in my own mind.'

'What would you like to know?'

Slim opened a packet of crisps he had pilfered from a basket in the guesthouse's breakfast room, ripped one edge and then spread them out on the table. He took one, offered them to Toby, and then said, 'What do you think happened? You've told me what you saw, now tell me what you think. Police work is always so much about evidence, but private investigators go on theories more than anything else, trying to spot an angle the police might have missed. Who was the man? Where did Jennifer go? Is she alive or dead?'

Toby took a crisp then looked down. 'Well. … this might sound stupid,' he said. 'It took me years before I even saw it, and even longer to come around to what it meant, but in the end it made perfect sense.'

'Try me.'

'There's a visitor in that picture.'

'A what?'

'A visitor.' Toby gave Slim an embarrassed grin. 'It's a term I use in my books. That picture's where the idea came from. A visitor is a person who isn't from this time and place.'

Slim suppressed a groan. 'So ... you mean like a time traveler?'

Toby nodded, then gave a frantic shake of his head. 'Yes, but also no. A visitor could be one of a number of things. A time traveler, or a spirit, or even an extraterrestrial. What's important is that they've been here.'

'Important?'

'Yes!' Toby had a huge grin on his face, but his voice held a tremble of fear. 'And their appearance upsets the fabric of what we know of reality.'

Had he not been sitting down, Slim night have been tempted to take a backward step. He had dealt with psychotics before and still had the scars. He had no intention of getting close to another.

'Go on. I'm still listening,' he said. *With half a barrel of salt*, he didn't add.

'When a visitor appears in our world, it can upset the balance of a great number of things. Time. Reality. Order.' Toby spread his hands. 'Look, you're probably thinking that I'm crazy. Here's the guy who writes books about magic and strange creatures wanting to be taken seriously about a woman's disappearance. But we once thought the world was flat, right?'

Slim shrugged. 'I imagine there are people who still do.'

'And we're nowhere near the peak of our intellectual

understanding. What I'm talking about is a pseudo-science, one that has a basis in fact but doesn't yet have the backing of the greater scientific community.'

Slim lifted his hand. 'Look, this is all very nice, but how do you think it's going to help me find Jennifer?'

Toby took a deep breath. 'Because I don't think she is lost. I think that in a certain reality, she's still right here.'

28

'A SPACE CADET,' SLIM SAID, TAKING A SIP OF COFFEE. 'Without question. And believe me, I've met my fair share of nut jobs. He kept talking about "visitors". If there was anyone who met that description, it was the man in front of me.'

Lia laughed. 'So I suppose his profession didn't surprise you?'

'He certainly has an imagination. Whether it would help with the case … at this stage I doubt it.'

Lia reached across the bar and patted Slim's hand, letting it linger a little too long to be casual. Slim met her eyes and felt a momentary hesitation at what he saw there. Lia actually seemed to like him, something that in its very unlikeliness made Slim uncomfortable. Enjoying it gave him the same sort of guilt as when he turned back to the bottle, and he found it hard not to draw his hand away.

'Don't give up,' she said. 'I have faith in you. Oh—' she gave his hand another frantic tap, '—my friend spoke to her great uncle again. Robert Downs? He said he's willing to talk to you again.'

'That would be great.'

'Apparently he felt bad about the way he treated you. He said you caught him unawares with what you wanted to know. She said she'll call me later.'

'Excellent news. Our conversation was somewhat stunted last time. It's my fault really. I should have been straight with him from the start.'

They talked for a short while longer before Slim excused himself to go and make some calls. Standing on the street outside, he returned a missed call from Kim.

'Good morning, Mr. Hardy,' she said, sounding full of cheer. 'Great news. I got in touch with Manchester Piccadilly as per your request and was told you would be welcome to come down and have a look at the train that used to run on the Hope Valley Line back in the seventies. I spoke to the goods yard's caretaker, but he couldn't give me much detail on the train's condition, only that while it had been used for parts, it was mostly intact. He said you were welcome to come down and take a look any time. He said he would gladly show you around.'

Slim couldn't keep the smile off his face. 'That's fantastic news.'

'Oh, and I'm on to book four of Firth's series. I have to say, it's quite gripping.'

Slim rolled his eyes. 'Like the man himself, no doubt.'

The day was looking up. Slim almost felt like whistling as he strolled down the high street to the station and turned onto the old bridleway leading alongside the tracks.

It was a pleasant day, sunny but not too hot, as he set off to walk again to Wentwood. This time, however, as he walked, he wasn't looking at the path but at the railway tracks, wondering what secrets could be told by those shiny, humming rails.

The other side of the tracks was mostly fields once you were past the town's brief suburbs. A few small level crossings allowed for easy passage to the other side, some doubling up as little bridges that crossed a stream gurgling along the same valley route as the railway line. About halfway to Wentwood, Slim took a narrow lane leading over the tracks and climbed a hill leading up to an area of open moorland, from where he had a panoramic view of the valley below. He found a bench in a layby and sat down to eat a sandwich and take a swig from a flask of coffee. A middle-aged couple waved as they jogged past, all luminous dress and reflective armbands, and Slim felt a sudden craving for the kind of carefree existence they appeared to have.

But what was under the surface? Every lake had monsters of one kind or another. Perhaps the man distributed child porn, or the woman had broken up her boss's family. No appearance could be trusted. No cover truly represented its contents.

The train line from Holdergate to Wentwood hid its own monster, Slim knew, and it was slowly bubbling to the surface. He could feel it.

29

HE CALLED KAY THE NEXT MORNING BUT WAS TOLD TO wait a little longer. Kay had managed to find a friend who worked in the photographic industry to examine the copies Slim had passed him, but Kay was yet to hear back. After ending the call, Slim headed for the station and took a train to Manchester. There, as before, he assumed the guise of Mike Lewis and planted a few more seeds in the homeless community.

He was on the last train back, leaning wearily against the window when his phone rang. Toby's name came up on the screen and Slim reluctantly answered, feigning enthusiasm as he said, 'Hello?'

'I was wondering whether to tell you,' Toby said. 'Actually, I'd planned to, but you never called.'

'Sorry, I had business in Manchester. An interview.'

He'd been told to take a hike by more people than those who'd been prepared to listen, but Slim wasn't about to tell Toby that. He was demoralised enough by being spat on, threatened with a broken arm, and told he'd better be watching his back at all times to want to relive it in a conversation.

'Oh, anything interesting?' Toby's tone was furtive, bordering on insistent.

'Had to see a man about a dog.'

'But not a man about a ghost?'

'What?'

'I wanted to tell you, but it seemed stupid.'

Slim rolled his eyes. As though Toby had told him anything that wasn't. 'Tell me what?'

'About the Holdergate ghost.'

'Look, it's been a long day.'

'I just thought it might be something of interest.'

Slim suppressed a sigh. 'Sure. Go ahead, I'm listening.'

'I grew up in Chapel-en-le-Frith, a few miles from here. When we were in primary, you know how kids are and all that, a monster behind every hedge and everything … we used to tell stories to scare each other. Especially after school, you know, we'd always be trying to one-up each other.'

'Yes, I remember.'

'And by then I was into my books, scribbling down stories, hiding them in my locker at school because … well, it doesn't matter now, but anyway … and word got around that Holdergate had a ghost. Some kid from my class said you'd hear him screaming late at night in the goods yard behind the station.'

'Right. But you never heard him yourself?'

'No, of course not. I'd never even been to Holdergate except that one time. But I always wondered if it wasn't who I caught in that picture, you know, the Holdergate ghost. I mean, you remember what I said about visitors?'

Slim pulled his phone away from his ear and lifted his

finger. He could easily cut Toby off, then blame a tunnel or the weather at a later time. It had been a long day.

Toby's tinny voice still came from the speaker, though, and Slim flinched at what sounded like a familiar word.

'Wait, say that again.'

'I said, I mean, what if it was Tom I got on camera? If you could find a historical photo of him, if there was some way to enhance the image—'

'Wait, wait—Tom?'

'Yeah, that's what this kid from school said the ghost's name was. The ghost of some boy who died during the station's construction, something like that. Tom Jedder.'

30

TOBY HAD LITTLE EXTRA TO SAY IN PERSON. HE FLAPPED his hands around a lot and waxed lyrical as perhaps only a born storyteller could, but while he still remembered the name of Tom Jedder and some of the tall tales and playground taunts they had sung, he could no longer remember who had originally told him the name. Going on the hearsay of a professional novelist was not Slim's preferred mode of operation, but with no concrete leads, he was prepared to allow Toby a little indulgence.

'I must have been eight or nine,' Toby said, waving around a capped styrofoam coffee cup as though it were an extension of his hand. 'You know? When I first heard it. Those were back in the Peak District Strangler days, when we would go home in groups, the last kid on the walk home being picked up from the second-to-last kid's house. Didn't matter that the victims were all women; there was a constant fear that the Strangler might change his tastes. Even after they caught him it carried on, in case the police had picked up the wrong man. No one in a school's management wanted blood on his hands.'

'I would expect not.'

Toby smiled. 'Of course, we played up to it. It became commonplace to leave kids behind, run off when someone stopped to check his bag, the usual juvenile stuff. Our parents would have belted our hides had they known, but as long as it was all smoothed out before we got to the last house on the home route, we got away with it.' He shrugged. 'The name though, I always thought that came because we didn't have a name for the Strangler at that time, and also he became a ghost haunting the railway line because little kids didn't really understand the significance of a man murdering prostitutes. I didn't even know what sex was back then.'

'But you all knew the railway line?'

'Of course. It was the centre of our existence. In the case of many of us, quite literally. It ran through the middle of town and we were constantly crossing it to play at friends' houses. We used to wait for the trains, race them, sometimes play chicken.'

'Play chicken? You don't mean what I think you mean?'

Toby shrugged. 'Yeah, well it wasn't all the time, just once in a while. I never did it, but a few of the tough kids did. Impress their mates, that kind of thing.'

'Interesting.'

'Come to think of it, the name of Tom Jedder might have come from that.' Toby laughed. 'You know, like a kid who died playing chicken, something like that.'

'I'll have a look into it.'

'Of course, it was a long time ago and my memory isn't always as clear as I'd like. It was kid stuff. No phones or computers in those days.'

'I remember.'

'It all kind of died a death after a driver complained,' Toby continued. 'Someone from the station got in touch with the school for the addresses of us local kids, then came door knocking, telling us all to pack it in.' Toby gave a nervous laugh, and Slim instantly recognised the grown up kid who had blubbered to him on their first night together. 'God, I got a hammering for that. Guilty by association, I suppose.'

Slim said nothing. Toby stared off into space, fingers twitching nervously.

'So, anyway, I always thought that maybe a ghost got her.'

'Jennifer?'

'Yes. But ghosts don't kill people do they? They only scare them. They might make them run away, though. What if Tom Jedder scared Jennifer so badly that she went away and never came back, or worse, scared her into another place entirely?'

31

'OKAY, KIM, THIS IS THE DRILL. I NEED YOU TO contact as many people on that list as possible and ask them what they know about him. It's for a possible documentary, a kind of *This is Your Life*. For this reason, you need to make it clear from the outset that it's to be kept quiet.'

'Okay ... and what specifically are you looking for me to find out?'

'I'm trying to track down old primary school friends of Toby. And this might sound strange, but I'm looking for people who remember him in a negative light. If anyone makes any offhand comment—he was a strange kid, that kind of thing—make a note of it.'

'Okay, Mr. Hardy. I'll be sure to do that.'

Slim hung up the call and took a sip of his coffee. Investigating Toby's background made him uncomfortable, but it felt important to get a second opinion on the man's character. The writer felt untrustworthy, but Slim felt that if he could strip away the man's layers of imagination he might find a nugget of truth hidden beneath.

Slim finished his coffee and headed out. He took a bus rather than waiting for a train because the bus route meandered through the hills, passing through numerous outlying villages before dropping back into each town. It gave him a different perspective, an alternative view of the countryside, setting free thoughts and ideas that the stuffiness of a town left undeveloped.

He got off at a quiet stop on Wentwood's outskirts and walked the rest of the way to Webster's Home for the Elderly.

'I hope Barnard will be comfortable talking to me,' Slim told a receptionist, once more assuming the guise of Mike Lewis, BBC researcher. 'I assure you that I only want to talk to him about what he remembers. I'm happy for a member of staff to be present.' It was necessary to say so to get through the door, but he hoped she would wave it off. When she nodded and agreed, however, his expectations sank.

'If you go along the corridor to consultation room number three, I'll have a nurse bring Mr. Litchfield down.' She handed him an ID card on a string to put around his neck. On the card, GUEST was written in large blue letters. 'There's a coffee machine at the end of the corridor.' She gave him a sympathetic smile. Slim was wondering if his natural demeanor made him look tired when the woman added, 'It can sometimes take a while to get the residents organised.'

Slim did as she suggested. He was on his second cup when Litchfield came through the door in a wheelchair pushed by a young nurse whose name tag identified him as CALL ME DAN. He settled Litchfield into position on one side of the table, then came around and whispered to Slim, 'Keep the questions simple, and if he goes off on a tangent just let him run with it. Some days he's there, some days he's not.'

Litchfield coughed. 'If you've finished your damn mother's meeting over there could we get on with this?'

Dan smiled. 'If he curses it means he's feeling good. You'll get more out of him than gibberish.'

'Hurry up over there, you useless prick,' Litchfield said. 'My colostomy bag's pinching.'

Slim sensed from the way Dan smiled in response that their camaraderie came with a mutual respect. Dan gave Litchfield a genial pat on the back, adjusted what needed to be adjusted, and then nodded at Slim to begin.

'I'm sorry to be bothering you again, Mr. Litchfield,' he said. 'But I've got a little further in my research—'

Litchfield lifted a hand. 'Excuse me, lad, but who are you again?'

Slim glanced at Dan, who shrugged. 'Well, my name is Mike Lewis…' he began, then proceeded to roll off the usual spiel he used when masquerading as a BBC researcher. He closed by reminding Litchfield of their previous meeting. 'And I really wanted to ask you to expand on some of your comments.'

'Aye,' Litchfield said. 'You remind me of me old brother's lad,' he said. 'Sam. You have his eyes. How was that clay I got you for Christmas that year? Bet it surprised your dad when Uncle Barn showed up, didn't it?'

Slim frowned, but Dan gave him a discreet wave to indicate he should go with Litchfield's narrative, so he leaned forward and nodded.

'Yeah, it did. Those were good days, weren't they?'

'The best,' Litchfield growled. His thorny old face brightened with a smile which abruptly died. 'Until your old man started throwing his lies about. Didn't see you much after that. You know I never did nothing with your ma, don't you? Fool never wondered how she paid for everything, but I wasn't one of her punters. He might have figured it out sooner, but he always gave a pint glass more attention than he ever gave her.'

Slim forced a laugh. 'I was a kid, just enjoying myself. Say, you remember that dog we used to play with? The one by the tracks? I wonder what ever happened to that old mutt.'

Litchfield shrugged. 'Damned if I know. Got hungry and ran off, I imagine.'

Slim took a deep breath, preparing to play his hand. If he got it wrong and Litchfield closed up, the information he hoped for might never be revealed.

'He was Jedder's dog, wasn't he? Tom Jedder.'

Litchfield nodded. 'Aye, he was.'

Dan had begun to frown as though Slim was getting close to a line he shouldn't cross, but Slim pressed on. 'Jedder, he lived up the street, didn't he?'

Litchfield flapped a hand, then laughed. 'Boy, your memory's worse than mine. Jedder, that pitiful swine, he spent more time walking up and down those tracks than he ever did in a proper home. No one much wanted him around, used to berate him something like if he was ever seen about. But you know, Jedder, he wasn't no harm to anyone, even with that face, not unless you're trying to sleep at any rate. I suppose that's why he got given that dog. Finally had something that could love him.'

Litchfield chuckled, so Slim chuckled along with him. 'I wonder what happened to Jedder in the end.'

Litchfield leaned forward, a frown on his wizened old face. 'When did you and your ma leave town? Eighty-two?'

Slim shrugged. 'Ah … I suppose it was about then.'

'Figures. You wouldn't have been about when it happened.'

'What happened?'

'When they found him. On the tracks.' Litchfield shrugged. 'What was left of him at any rate.'

Slim caught a glance from Dan and sensed the nurse was getting ready to shut the conversation down. As Dan fidgeted and cleared his throat, Slim quickly said, 'An accident?'

'Nah.' Litchfield chuckled. 'Not a chance.'

'Mr. Litchfield, I think—'

'Put a sock in it. I'm talking with my brother.'

Unsure at what point his family status had changed, Slim simply gave Dan a shrug and leaned forward.

'Awful business, that.'

'Yeah. You know whoever did it was watching. Maybe the first time didn't kill him, I don't know, but they dragged him back on, finished him off. Covered him up both times with firs so the drivers wouldn't call it in. Filthy business that.'

'I suppose they never caught who did it.'

'Aye. I always thought it was your lad Sam. Went off the rails, didn't he?' Litchfield suddenly guffawed. 'Mind the pun.'

'Ah, he's okay these days.'

Litchfield frowned. 'Is that so? I thought he went belly up in mid eighty-five. Your old dear came up and drove me down for the funeral. Are you sure you're who you say you are?'

As Litchfield leaned forward again, Slim wondered if he'd been exposed, but the old man muttered, 'Ted, is that you? Your hair's looking grey. How's trade up the shop these days? That bloody Tescos put you out of business yet?'

Attempts to get Litchfield back on track proved fruitless, so after another ten minutes of rambling during which Slim tried to look interested, he made his excuses, thanked Litchfield and headed out. At the main exit, Dan caught up with him.

'I trust you'll be careful about what you use for your program,' he said, and Slim made a mental note to remember he was still playing a character.

'Of course,' he said. 'I imagine most of what he said was mere rambling. I couldn't use anything unless it was independently verified,' he said.

As he left the building, however, he felt certain that somewhere within Litchfield's words was a major clue.

32

'A BODY ON THE TRACKS?' LIA SAID, SHRUGGING AS SHE sipped her drink. 'I'll ask my mum if she remembers anything.'

'I don't think I'll say anything to Robert tomorrow,' Slim said. 'Not after how he reacted last time.'

'He might be okay about that one,' Lia said. 'It sounds like it was out along the line somewhere, and a homeless person wouldn't have gained as much press as Jennifer did. Most of the local papers keep one eye on the tourism industry. Believe it or not, unexplained disappearances are gold. They draw people in, but murders scare them away.'

Slim nodded. 'I could quite believe it,' he said.

'Sadly, there are several jumpers along the Hope Valley Line every year,' Lia said. 'I think a lot of desperate people choose somewhere pretty to spend their last moments. However, you hardly ever read about them in the papers. I hear from Robert via my friend, but only because he used to work at the station and still keeps in touch with the current station master.'

After finishing lunch, Slim left Lia to her work and

headed back to Wentwood and the library. There, on a microfiche of a newspaper from 1982, Slim found a brief article. Less than a hundred words long, it was tucked into a corner of the *Chronicle*'s fourth page, hidden next to an advert for a tractor wholesaler, in as missable place as it was possible to be.

BODY FOUND ON TRACKS

The body of an unidentified male was found on the tracks of the Hope Valley Line just south of the Clifford Road level crossing. His body was discovered by a dog walker. The likely cause of death was given as an impact wound. According to a police spokesman, the death is not at this stage being treated as suspicious. The investigation continues.

Slim searched forward a few months but could find no more mention of the death. He made a note to ask Charles Bosworth the next time they spoke. Then he changed tack, looking for any entries under the name of Tom Jedder.

He had quickly figured the name was likely fake, a nickname maybe taken from some local source. There were no newspaper articles in the years surrounding the homeless man's death, so Slim instead logged on to a computer database and did an online search.

There he found a historical reference: Thomas Jedder was the name of a local boy who had drowned in the river alongside the old bridleway round the turn of the last century, having presumably fallen in while leading a horse pulling a barge loaded with ore from one of the old mines. His existence in history had been reduced to a footnote in a local mining encyclopedia, and there was no mention anywhere of a ghost. The name was a coincidence, perhaps, but it was also a line of enquiry that was leading Slim farther and farther from Jennifer's trail.

After finishing up in the library, he headed back to Manchester, where again he spent the early evening distributing his phone number among the local homeless population, this time along with the name of Tom Jedder as a reference. Without any leads so far, it was looking like a fruitless exercise. He'd received no calls, and had begun to encounter the same faces over again, many of which were no happier to see him than they had been the first time.

Aware he was quickly gaining an unwanted reputation in Manchester's alleyways, he caught an earlier train than usual and headed back to Holdergate.

Instead of going straight back to his lodgings, he turned right out of the station, following a narrow road which meandered in roughly the same direction as the train line until he saw the lights of a level crossing appear out of the dark. Here, he climbed over a barrier and walked along the tracks with only the moonlight to guide him. He estimated the distance from the crossing where Litchfield claimed Tom Jedder's body had been found, and when he reached it he stopped and sat down beside the tracks, letting the atmosphere of this desolate place soak into him, and wondering both who the homeless man and the person who had lain his body on the tracks might have been.

33

'LOOK, MR. ... UM, HARDY? I'M AFRAID YOU'RE NOT really following correct procedure by just showing up and asking to speak to any nurse over a certain age. We're busy. It would have been more appropriate to call ahead.'

Slim gave the staff nurse the most pathetic smile he could muster. 'I know that, and I'm sorry. I'm just so desperate for information that I thought I'd stop by, just on the off-chance someone remembered.'

'What is it exactly?'

Slim took a deep breath, rehearsing the backstory he had scribbled down in the margin of a discarded newspaper on the train from Holdergate.

'My grandmother recently died, and in her will there was a note about a child she had from a previous marriage my mother had never known about. It left a quite substantial amount of money to be put toward the proper burial of the son in question, who died sometime in 1977, according to my grandmother. Apparently he died here, on the cancer ward. She gave only a first name, Jim.'

The staff nurse shrugged. 'Look, this is a quite fanciful

story. Come up to the staff room and we'll see if anyone has any clue what you're talking about.'

Slim followed the nurse, who gave her name as Sue, up to a plain common room where several members of staff sat around eating or drinking. One or two wore the weary expressions of people at the end of their shift, while a few others looked about to begin.

Sue called them to attention and introduced Slim. He stuffed his hands in his pockets and gave a sheepish grin.

'Go on, tell them what you told me,' Sue said.

Slim repeated his story, directing it at the older workers in the group. A few shrugged and a few others shook their heads. 'Perhaps I could just leave a contact number?' he said, taking out his wallet and withdrawing a few copies of the simplified version of his business card which featured just his name and phone number.

As he smiled and started to back out of the room, one of the younger nurses picked it up, squinted at his name, and then let out a squeal of delight.

'Oh, I knew it! Slim Hardy! I saw you on the TV.'

Disinterested faces suddenly seemed interested. A few random questions fired his way, but Slim brushed them off. Then Sue said, 'Mr. Hardy, did you just spin us a line?'

'No ... I, ah, I have to go. I have an appointment.'

'It's him!' the young nurse gushed. 'He's a famous detective.'

'Actually, I'm a private investigator.'

Sue and a couple of others were rolling their eyes. Slim had started to sweat, so he backed out of the room and hurried for the nearest lift. He made it, only to find Sue at his shoulder, eyes glowering. The lift opened and she bundled him inside.

'I'll just make sure you find the way out,' she snapped.

'Just in case you were thinking to waste any more of our time.'

Luckily for Slim, there were two other people in the lift. Sue glared at him all the way to the ground floor, and then walked with him until the main entrance came into view.

'Good luck with your investigation or whatever you're doing,' she snapped, leaving him to walk the last part of the way on his own. Slim glanced back and saw Sue waving to a security guard as he made his rounds.

He walked down the street and turned the first corner that took him out of sight of the hospital. The second building he passed was a dingy pub called the Duck and Crown. Slim found himself sitting on a bar stool with a pint in front of him yet no memory of the words passing his lips. He stared at the amber liquid, frowning until his brow hurt, fingers trembling on his knees. He sensed another turning of the wheel, another cycle about to begin.

He had followed this road so many times. He had broken the cycle, repaired himself, only to find the taint still there, hiding beneath the surface. Sooner or later the layers above would be stripped away and Slim's illness would be laid bare, grinning up at him, skeletal hands reaching out to plunge him back down into its inky depths. And he would struggle and fight and perhaps get his head back above water, but one day, he knew, the strength to fight would no longer be there, and it would claim him.

The smell was intoxicating. Slim's eyes watered, his vision blurred. His head pounded and he gritted his teeth, holding in a scream that rattled at the back of his throat, fighting to get out.

He couldn't do this. He couldn't keep fighting. The

strength was no longer there, and he couldn't handle it alone.

He needed help.

Pulling out his phone, he called the first number that appeared, and when a woman's voice answered, he opened his mouth to speak, but no sound would come out. All he could do was mouth two words:

Help me.

34

IT WAS NIGHT, BUT HE DIDN'T KNOW WHAT TIME. HE WAS lying on the ground next to a park bench, and from the ache in his side it was clear he had rolled off, perhaps catching the sloping corner of a concrete foot post on the way. His phone lay beneath him, jammed into a crack in the concrete. The casing had gained a couple of scratches but the rest of his indestructible Nokia was intact. And charged. He marveled at this miracle of engineering and design as he opened the display to find seven missed calls from Lia. His vision blurred as he squinted at her name, then his stomach contracted and he vomited between his feet.

'Oi, muppet!' came a shout from nearby. Slim looked up to see three young men strutting across the park, all baseball caps, trainers, and untucked dress shirts. 'I'll clean your shoes for fifty quid!' Then they were gone in a calamitous cackle of discordant laughter, passing through a gate onto a road.

Slim tried to get up but slipped back down, so gave up and just sat with his back against the bench seat. He tried to remember what had happened, but it appeared he had blacked out. He remembered leaving the hospital and entering the pub, ordering a drink … then nothing. He didn't remember if he had even begun drinking it.

He felt strange, as though he hadn't really gone on a binge at all, but had rather walked into a place and emerged in a different one entirely. Was this what Toby meant about visitors? Was it just a lyrical way to describe alcoholics and other misfortunates on society's fringes stumbling through a life that had no need for them? Was he visiting now, sitting in some alternative reality while in another time and place a different man calling himself John "Slim" Hardy was living an entirely more fulfilling existence?

The temptation to just give up and turn himself over to his urges was momentarily overwhelming. It was probably not so late that there wasn't a bar open somewhere nearby which would take his credit card, or a late night newsagent, or failing that, somewhere with a window fragile enough to be broken in. As the urge passed, however, he found that the difficulty of getting up outweighed his desire to drink and drink and drink until there was nothing left but a fizzing puddle where a man had once stood.

He sighed, his head lolling, and through a blur as his eyes faltered once again he saw a man waving as he approached Slim from across the park.

The concern that this was a lout looking for a face to kick was immediately extinguished by a friendly smile surrounded by the polyester fur of a duffel coat. Slim sat up as the man slung a rucksack off his shoulder and opened it in the same moment, demonstrating an action he had clearly performed hundreds of times before.

'I have sandwiches, but I also have one burger left. Still hot. It's cold out, isn't it?'

The man sat down on the bench, leaning over Slim like a father leaning over a child who had fallen in mud. Slim took the offered bundle of greaseproof paper and felt a welcome warmth emanating from inside. He didn't remember when he had last eaten, but it was likely sometime before he started to drink.

'Do you have any water?' he asked, realising his throat was parched.

'I have hot soup,' the man said, producing a flask. 'Well, it's not "hot" hot, but there should be a bit of warmth left.'

'Thanks.'

Slim took the offered cup and took a long swallow, immediately feeling better. The urge to continually drink was slowly dying, leaving him left with the aftermath of a savage binge from which to begin to rebuild. It was possible. He had done it before.

'I haven't seen you before,' the man said. 'How long have you been out here?'

'I'm not sure.'

'Couldn't you get to a shelter?' The man glanced up. 'It's clear now, but it's going to rain soon. It could be rough out here in a couple of hours. Where are your things?'

Slim looked around him, frowning, then suddenly realised what the man had assumed.

'I'm not—' he began, but the man put up a hand.

'It's all right. If you tell me where I'm likely to find you, I can send someone to assess you. There are programs. I'm guessing it's the drink. You don't look a substance user.'

'I'm not.'

'Well, that's something.'

'Look, I know what this looks like, but I'm not homeless. I mean, I have been in the past, but I'm not now. I just had some trouble, that's all. I … relapsed.'

The man was nodding as though he still didn't believe Slim, but he stuck out a hand and said, 'My name's Terry Denton. I run Giving, a homeless charity. What's your name?'

'John Hardy. But people call me Slim.'

They shook hands. Terry frowned. 'Sounds familiar— wait! You're that guy. The one who's been wandering around asking questions. Several of my regulars have mentioned you. Caused quite a stir, you have. What on earth happened to you?'

'I relapsed. Other than that, I'm not quite sure.'

'Well, you're still in one piece, by the look of things. That's a decent start. Do you drink coffee?'

Slim couldn't help but laugh. 'Of course,' he said. 'I drink as much of it as I can.'

35

THE CLOCK BEHIND THE MAN CHOPPING CABBAGE AT A counter read 3 a.m. Slim faced Terry Denton across the Formica tabletop of the late-night greasy spoon, a steaming cup of long-overbrewed coffee in front of each.

'You understand the rules of the street,' Terry said.

Slim nodded. 'You either get off it or you die.'

'Or you keep going back,' Terry added with a wry smile. 'Took me ten years to get off it for good, and I faced my maker a number of times. In the end, though, I had a little more gumption than he did. Been forty years since I got out of the gutter, but the pain of it stays with me every day. That's why I founded Giving. Every time I help someone back to their feet, the buzz … I mean, I don't know what people are getting high on these days, but it's like no drug I ever took.'

Slim smiled. 'I can understand,' he said. 'I think the only thing that makes me feel better than a night on the bottle is solving a crime.' His smile faded, and he sighed. 'It's a shame the journey is so hard.'

'Never stop fighting,' Terry said. 'Once a demon has its

claws in you, there's no shaking it off. I don't care what anyone says. You'll never be free once you have the taint.'

'You seem to have done all right.'

'Because I face what could be again every single day,' Terry said. 'I work the graveyard shift, midnight until dawn, most nights. That's when you see the worst things, those closest to the edge. In their eyes I see my own, over and over again. You want to break the cycle? Go work with the worse drinkers you can find. Not bingers or functionals, but those who could literally die on their next drink. There's your cure right there.'

'Maybe I'll try it.'

'You're young enough yet to do it. Now, tell me what brought you to a park bench at two in the bloody morning and let me see if it adds up to what I've heard.'

'I'm looking for a homeless man who died in the cancer ward of Manchester Royal Infirmary in January 1977, the same night that a young nurse disappeared from Holdergate Station, leaving no trace, and was never seen or heard from again. Is there anything I've said that you can help me with?'

Terry Denton reached into his pocket and pulled out a packet of cigarettes. He shrugged as Slim lifted an eyebrow. 'Let an old man keep one vice,' Terry said, standing up. 'Give me five minutes. Then I'll tell you what I know.'

36

'It's perfect,' Kay said. 'Are you looking at it right now?'

Slim held up the picture with one hand, angling it to the light, pressing his phone to his ear with his other. 'I still don't see it.'

'Clearly the kid had no idea what he was doing, but he's lined it up with such accuracy that my friend was astonished,' Kay said. 'Polaroids have a longer exposure than a regular camera, and any further movement would have blurred it too much for the figure to be seen, making it clearly the result of a superimposed image. As it is, it's just clear enough that you can be fooled into thinking it's just that one man.'

Slim frowned. 'As a layman, run it by me again. What exactly am I seeing?'

'The boy is standing a few feet inside a window. According to my friend, the room would have been in near darkness, perhaps a corridor or porch, otherwise the reflection would have been more prominent. As it is, most of the other signs of it are hidden among the trees at the top or the buildings on either side. He's taken a picture of the street, and both a man and Jennifer Evans can be seen, but the reason the man appears fractionally blurred is because a reflection of another man almost perfectly covers him. It's not a direct reflection however, or the image would have been too large. According to my friend, such a situation could have been caused by a secondary reflection in a slightly angled surface such as a mirror. This in turn is projecting an image on to something behind the boy holding the camera, something more likely stainless steel, which has both reduced and resized the original to exactly match the size and stature of the man standing in the street. It's frankly remarkable.'

'A reflection of another person is overlaying the man standing by the park?'

'That's exactly it. It's so accurate it has to have been a million in one fluke chance.'

Slim nodded, but still couldn't see it, despite what Kay said. 'Is it possible to separate the two images so they might be identified?'

'My friend is working on it. He said he'll get back to me in a day or two. He couldn't guarantee that he could produce anything worthwhile, but he said to wait and see.'

'Thanks, Kay. Did your friend have anything to say about the supposed missing footprints?'

'That, he said, is likely to have a far more rational explanation. A trick of angles, most likely, or shadows. He said he couldn't be sure unless he visited the spot in question, but that the answer would most likely be found there.'

'Thanks, Kay. That's great.'

'Anytime, Slim. You know that.'

Slim hung up. He slipped his phone back into his

pocket and headed for Holdergate Station. There, he climbed the steps to the main building and went through a side door into the waiting room. It was modernised now, all glass and Perspex, with advertising hoardings blocking the view from the spot where Toby would have stood to take his picture.

At an information desk, a busy clerk waved off his request for any pictures of the original layout, telling him to visit the local library or the village museum. With time to kill before meeting Robert in the evening, Slim went outside and walked up the street to Holdergate Park. A railing fence lined the outside, with entrances on each of four corners. Two crossing diagonal paths created the main layout with smaller paths leading off to neat flower gardens, a children's playground, and a small boating lake.

Slim went inside at the corner nearest the station, then backtracked to the section of fence where the man shown in the photograph had been standing and examined the fence and the park layout from inside. He quickly found himself frowning. An old stone flowerbed along the inside had two sections of wall clearly of different ages. To the right it was crumbling and devastated by lichen, but on Slim's left was modern stonework, the concrete showing only a few hairline cracks. Slim estimated it to be about twenty years old, suggesting this section of the flowerbed was part of a more recent renovation. The left part of the fence appeared newer than the section by the old flowerbed wall, still with its original dark green paintwork, rather than the clearly painted-over rust patches of the older part.

Confident he already had the answer he was looking for, Slim took a walk across the park and found an aging gardener repairing a section of path disrupted by tree roots. After introducing himself as a former Holdergate resident who hadn't been back to the area in many years, Slim enquired as to why the park had been restructured. The gardener, apparently thankful for a reason to take a break from the painstaking task of levering up sections of tarmac and sawing through the roots pushing up from beneath, pulled off his gloves and waved Slim to follow as he headed across the grass.

'Council got funding back in ninety-three,' he said. 'Put that playground in over there, added that fountain and the skate park the kids round here are too posh to use, relaid the paths and replaced part of the old perimeter fence.'

'Was there an old entrance directly opposite the station?'

The gardener nodded. 'Used to be, but the council voted to have it closed up. Poor layout design. Everyone used to walk across the grass to get to it, leaving ugly patches of earth. Now they have to use the path.' He pointed at the section of fence Slim had examined a few minutes before. 'Because of the slight slant of the road, two sections of fence overlapped. When they removed the entrance, they actually widened part of the pavement to make the fence look straight.'

Slim pulled copies of Toby's photos out of his pocket and unfolded them. He showed the gardener.

'This picture was taken second,' he said, pointing to the picture showing only Jennifer's footprints. 'Would the old gate have made it possible for the man to appear to vanish without leaving any tracks?'

The gardener squinted. 'Don't really know my photography, but whoever took this is standing at an angle which makes the two parts of the fence look continuous. Also the light's poor and you've got that snow … but if you look at the spikes of the railings, they've a slight discrepancy in their heights, showing these to the left are slightly in front of those to the right. Then there's this tree there—' he reached out and patted the trunk of a towering beech tree that loomed over them, '—and he's right to the left of it, which is exactly where the fence overlapped.'

'The man who took this says the man in the photo disappeared without leaving any tracks.'

'Did he walk up here and check?'

'I don't believe so.'

The old gardener laughed. 'Then I'd say he probably should have. I imagine he would have found a line of tracks leading away across the park.'

'I MUST APOLOGISE FOR MY REACTION LAST TIME YOU visited,' Robert Downs said, offering Slim the same seat he had used a few nights before Robert had abruptly got up and walked inside. 'It's just that I get more excited by people interested in trains than by people dredging up unpleasant memories.'

'It wasn't my intention to upset you. I never wanted that. Sometimes it's hard to know how something from so long ago might affect people in the periphery.'

Robert made a strange gesture of pulling back his head as though trying to draw his chin into his neck. Then he said, 'I can understand how your line of work might require you to enter some difficult situations.'

Slim thought about the scars hidden beneath his clothes as well as the worse ones that sometimes woke him shivering at night. He shrugged. 'Some days are harder than others.'

'So what would you like to know about Jennifer Evans? I can tell you what I told the police that night if you haven't already read their files.'

If Robert had been interviewed in connection with the disappearance, there had been nothing among the files Slim had seen. He made a note to ask Charles at their next meeting.

'I would appreciate it. I understand that the likelihood of finding Jennifer is remote, but I'm hoping to find something the police might have missed. If I could just ask you to tell me what you remember of that night, it would be a great help.'

Robert looked like he had been asked to swallow something unpleasant. Slim expected him to refuse, but at last Robert nodded.

'You know about the snow that week, I presume?' At Slim's nod, Robert continued, 'I've never seen a blizzard like it, before or since. At about half past eight I got the call from a maintenance crew working farther up the line that it was drifting so deep we risked a derailment if we allowed trains to continue. I called Sheffield and requested a locomotive fitted with a plow be sent up, but it wouldn't arrive until midnight, so the earliest we could consider the line safe was one a.m.'

Robert paused as a door opened and his partner appeared with a tray of tea and biscuits. She held back the pleasant smile Slim had previously received, glaring at him as though he had given her husband a heart condition. Robert waited patiently until she had put down the tray and gone back inside before he began to speak again.

'We had three trains due to pass through that night. I'm not sure what you know about stations, but Holdergate is fairly small. It was lucky, actually, because Holdergate is the only station with a goods yard on the Hope Valley Line between Manchester and Sheffield. It was us or leave them out in the open. We put the first train—a local from

Manchester—on to siding track three. The second train—the one on which Jennifer Evans supposedly travelled—we let run onto the main platform. The third train, which reached us fifteen minutes later, was a freight. We put that on siding track number one, which was the only one long enough to hold it without blocking the main line. So, as you might imagine, there was pandemonium. Holdergate, even at peak times, rarely held more than a hundred passengers at any one time. Now we have five or six hundred milling about. A number of local residents stepped up to help out—we had vats of soup brought in, heaters, paraffin for the stoves. After a while people stopped worrying and started to make a party spirit out of it. There was singing and dancing, the atmosphere was electric. I woke up the next morning sure I'd been involved in an evening that would go down as a local legend.' He leaned forward, resting his chin on his hands, staring off into the valley. 'Then a call comes in to say a young lady had gone missing.'

Slim said nothing, leaving the space open for Robert to continue. When the old man's silence began to make him uncomfortable, he said, 'You're angry, aren't you?'

Robert looked across as though remembering Slim were there.

'Yes,' he said. 'I am.'

'She ruined it for you, didn't she? She ruined Holdergate.'

Slim had expected several reactions, but not for Robert to start sobbing. He glanced around uncomfortably for any neighbours who might overhear, but the gardens on either side were empty, and the double-glazed windows into Robert's house were closed.

'That bitch,' Robert spat, his voice filled with so much

hate Slim was taken aback. 'Such a beautiful place. We never needed Jennifer Evans in our lives. She ruined everything.'

Slim didn't know where to look as Robert continued to cry. He chewed on a biscuit and finished his tea. Finally Robert looked up. He wiped his eyes, then shook his head as though trying to break free of the hold of a rather impish spirit.

'I do apologise for my reaction,' he said. 'I'm just an old man. I haven't thought about this in a long time and it brings back the most unpleasant thoughts.'

'I'm sorry if I'm making this hard for you,' Slim said. 'I have to ask, though. Did you see Jennifer Evans in the station that night?'

Robert gave a vehement shake of his head. 'No, I didn't. That night I saw no sign of her at all.'

38

'CAN I COME IN?'

Lia stood in the doorway, her mouth agape. 'I thought you'd shipped out of town until I got a call tonight from my friend to say you were around, distressing her great-uncle again. Do you know how worried I was about you? When you called and didn't speak, then you ignored my calls? What's the matter with you?'

Slim looked at the ground. 'I came to say I'm sorry. I screwed up again, so I buried myself in the case to get over it. I must have looked at your number a hundred times, but I didn't know what I'd say if you answered.'

'Are you drunk now?'

Slim chuckled. 'No, for once I'm not.'

'Well, I wish *I* was. I've never met anyone like you, Slim, that's for sure. I suppose you might as well come in. I'll let you try to explain.'

'Thank you.'

Lia stepped back as Slim ducked sheepishly through the door. She offered him a seat at the small kitchen table, then started to make coffee.

With her back turned, she said, 'Do you consider it normal to flit in and out of the lives of people who care for you? Is that generally how you operate?'

He sighed. 'Yes, it is. It's not intentional, but I've been alone for almost twenty years, and you could say even before that, depending how you look at it. I know no other way.'

Lia turned around and put a cup of coffee down in front of him. She was learning: it was black, and as thick as treacle. He was also sure she had stopped the kettle early so it wouldn't quite be piping hot.

She took a seat opposite but sat back, her arms folded, a defensive pose that brought flashbacks of prisoners who needed interrogation. Slim closed his eyes. Without opening them, he said, 'I came here to thank you for everything you've done for me, both as part of my case and for myself ... and to tell you that it would probably be best if we no longer saw each other.'

He opened his eyes. Lia was staring at him open-mouthed. As he watched, she let out a little laugh. 'Are you trying to break up with me? Isn't that a little presumptive considering we've only had, what? Two proper dates?'

'I think it would be bad for you to get too close to me,' he said. 'You've already seen much of the worst I have to offer. It won't get better.'

Lia frowned. 'How about you let me decide that for myself? I'm a grown woman, Slim. Believe it or not, for my past three boyfriends, I did the dumping. I can quite well decide when I've had enough.' She leaned forward. 'Unless, of course, you don't like me and you're trying to make an excuse?'

Slim felt his voice break as he said, 'Of course I like you. There's nothing not to like.'

'That's settled then.'

'What is?'

Lia reached across and took Slim's hands, which had somehow found their way to the tabletop. They were shaking, but for once he thought it was nerves, rather than from a craving for booze.

'We'll give it another try and see how it goes.'

'I'll only hurt you.'

'Like I said, let me judge that for myself.' She sat up suddenly. 'Let's put you though a little test. I haven't eaten yet, and I'm guessing you haven't either. I'll go and watch TV while you cook me dinner. You can only use what you can find in the kitchen, and don't touch my wine or it's all off.'

'Sure … can I use the phone or the microwave?'

Lia laughed. 'No!' She stood up. 'You have one hour. Your first task, however, is to make me another coffee.'

Slim stared at her back as she went through into her little living room and closed the door. Aware she both had the opportunity to save him or break herself trying to prevent him falling, he didn't know whether to laugh or cry.

39

'Here,' Terry Denton said, stepping off the path and indicating a small grave with his foot. A bunch of flowers in a metal pot were long dead. Terry pulled them out and tossed them away into the grass, then began picking the weeds away from the basic slate headstone.

'You left those?'

'I come by once a year or so. I visit a lot of old friends that way. Sometimes I think it's because I'm the only person who'll remember them. If they're still around somewhere, I'd like them to know that their lives weren't nothing, that they did exist, that they mattered.'

Slim nodded. Before meeting Lia, Slim had often felt like a walking member of this near-forgotten-drifter club.

'You knew Jim Randall from the streets?'

'And briefly before. We were both in and out of the social system during the early sixties. His parents, like mine, were both either unable to cope for one reason or another, or had too many children to deal with so passed a couple off to the system.' Terry shuddered. 'It was brutal in those days. You fitted in or you ended up on the streets or dead. We both did spells in and out of borstals, mostly for violence, vandalism. For a while we'd get factory work —legally you had to be sixteen, but no one cared if a fourteen-year-old fudged their papers up a few years—but it was hard for idle minds and the pay was crap. Easier and more fun to steal what you wanted, or flog things off to keep you going. It was easy to fall in with the wrong crowd, and once they were done lighting you up, they'd blow you out and leave you in a gutter somewhere.'

'Were you in contact at the time he died?'

Terry nodded. 'I'd got off the street by then and started to get back on my feet. It would be a few years before I founded Giving, but I was still in contact with a lot of the people I knew from those days. Many were my friends, and watching good men die … it broke me every time. But for circumstances….' Terry trailed off, shaking his head.

'I heard that he died of lung cancer.'

Terry was quiet for a moment. 'That's what we were told, yes.'

'You think it was something else?'

Terry frowned. 'I don't know you from Adam, Slim. But the effort you've gone to in this case … it makes me feel like I can trust you.'

'Trust me with what?'

'Something I've never told anyone. Something I never wanted to tell, not only because it was something you didn't do when you were on the street or because I was never asked the right questions … but because it always felt like a dirty thing to say. I tried to force it out of my mind. Cut it out, if you like.

'I saw him the day before he died, and went there the next day, expecting to see him again. I arrived to find he had died. The day before, he told me he was in a lot of

148

pain. It wasn't just cancer. He had syphilis, passed to him by his girlfriend at the time, who was a working girl, if you know what I mean. He was also malnourished, underweight. Both caused by years of hard living.'

Slim nodded. 'It left him too weak to fight the cancer, didn't it?'

'True. But the nurses I spoke to the day before told me he would last another month or two. That he died so suddenly suggested intervention.'

Slim had told Terry nothing about Jennifer. He had considered it, but during an investigation it was always better to keep your trump cards close. He thought about the best question to ask, aware that whatever Terry believed "dirty" was yet to be revealed.

'Did Jim ever tell you a name?' he asked slowly. 'Did he ever give you a clue who it might be? A girlfriend or a nurse, perhaps?'

Terry swallowed. He squatted down, his back to Slim, and at first Slim didn't realise he had pulled out a cell phone.

'It was a woman,' Terry said. 'That's all I can be sure about. However, my guess is she looked a little like this.'

He held up the phone to show Slim a composite photograph of four dark-haired young women in different poses. One was a sullen passport photograph. Another was of a girl holding a dog and grinning. The two others were posed against backgrounds which suggested bars or clubs. Slim had seen a photograph of Jennifer, and had to admit there was a resemblance.

'Who are these women?'

'Jean Casey. Barbara Shields. Tina Jones, and the last one is Emma Timpson.' Terry looked up. 'The four victims of the Peak District Strangler.'

40

'THEY WERE BROTHERS. RANDALL WASN'T JIM'S REAL last name, the same that Bettelman wasn't Jeremy's. They took their surnames from the last foster families which gave them a fixed address.'

'You think the Strangler killings were a revenge attack on the woman who supposedly helped Jeremy's brother to die.'

Terry nodded. 'Both that and revenge on the woman partly responsible for his illness. Jean Casey was Jim's girlfriend. It took Bettelman a year to track her down, but Jim was long dead and buried by then. The police never made the connection.'

'You didn't come forward?'

'I was barely off the streets. I, of course, had no idea Jeremy was responsible at the time, but I wasn't about to come forward with any names. It just wasn't done, and you didn't want Jeremy coming after you. He was a nasty piece of work if ever there was one. Growing up in those places does things to a man's personality.'

'You seem to have come through it okay,' Slim said.

'I gave up a lot more than life on the streets,' Terry said, his tone telling Slim that the old man had likely taken part in as many horrors as he had in Iraq.

Slim had a thousand more questions, but Terry had work to do, so they arranged to meet at a later date. Slim headed back to Holdergate, where he met Lia, who had just finished an early shift, in the Station Master for lunch. 'The Strangler,' he said, pulling from his pocket two pictures, one of Jennifer Evans in her nurse's uniform, another of the four victims he had printed from a shop near Manchester station.

'You think she was Bettelman's first victim?'

'When I saw the pictures of the murdered girls, it left me in little doubt, at least initially,' Slim said. 'I mean, the hair colour is the same, the approximate age at the time of death. A lot doesn't add up, though. If Jim Randall had told Jeremy about Jennifer, why the long delay between her death and his first recognised murder? He killed those four women in the space of six months, but there was over a year between Jennifer's disappearance and the first murder.'

'Perhaps there were others not recognised as his?'

'It's possible. I'll ask my secretary to dig up a list of unsolved murders from that period.'

'But you don't think so?'

'At this point, I have no proof of anything.'

Slim fell silent for a while as they ate. He sensed Lia watching him, and wondered how much of his theory he should reveal. The biggest problem was that if Jennifer had been murdered, where was the body?

The other victims of the Peak District Strangler had been left out in the open, almost as a taunt to the police, but of Jennifer there remained no trace.

41

'THANKS FOR AGREEING TO MEET ME,' SLIM TOLD THE grey-haired, bearded man sitting opposite him in the cafe outside Wentwood Station. 'To be honest, I wasn't sure anyone would respond to my request.'

The man, whose name was Peter Edwards, shrugged. 'Well, if you're going to make a program kissing his arse, at least get your facts straight.'

Edwards, according to Kim, had jumped at the chance to be interviewed for a possible TV program about the life of Tobin P. Firth. Slim had already sat through three pseudo-interviews with people who had proven to have barely known him at all, with most of their anecdotes little more than hearsay. One woman had shown up with her hair freshly done and then been upset that no TV cameras were present. Slim had explained to each that the interviews were speculative. On hearing this, the woman had given stunted answers to his first few questions and then cried off the rest of the interview, citing the sudden onset of a headache.

Edwards, on the other hand, appeared all too pleased to dish whatever dirt he had on his former classmate.

Propping a clipboard on his knee, Slim said, 'What do you remember about Tobin?'

Edwards rolled his eyes and scoffed. 'You mean Toby? Always made me laugh when I saw that name. Guy was full of himself.'

'At school, you mean? What kind of student was he?'

'"Lively" would be a polite way to put it. "A big-mouth," less so. Bit of a joker, liked to rile the older kids then run off laughing. He wasn't a fighter; always talked his way out of it, sometimes left his mates to get copped for it.'

'Was there much indication that he'd end up writing books for a living?'

Peter laughed. 'Oh yeah. He was constantly telling stories, many of which were elaborate lies. He never had a consistent circle of friends because he was always moving between groups. It made him hard to genuinely like, but it also felt like a popularity contest. He wanted to be the boy who knew everyone.'

'Did you like him?'

'Honestly?' Peter sighed. 'I didn't hate him. He was entertaining to be around, and always a laugh. But you couldn't trust a word that came out of his mouth. If you got on with him it was fine, but if you got on his bad side you'd suddenly hear rumours about yourself, like you had body odour, or you'd shagged the spotty girl everyone took the mick out of, or you'd been caught in the toilets with your dick in your hand and a copy of the class photo. No one would ever know quite where the rumour came from, but you could bet your life it started with Toby. Sometimes it seemed like he played school the way most people play video games these days. Like it was something to be won.'

Peter claimed to have last seen Toby aged fourteen, before Toby transferred schools to a different area of the county, but he had come with a contact for a woman called Denise Layman, whom he claimed had been a close friend of Toby's. Slim thanked him for coming, then headed back to his guesthouse to respond to some more voicemails.

Kim had left a message to say she had finished reading Toby's series, but when Slim called back she didn't answer. Probably gone to lunch, he assumed. Kay had also called but had left only a short message asking Slim to call him back. However, on Slim's attempt he got no answer, so instead he found himself penning a letter to Marjorie Clifford, thanking her for her letter and letting her know his progress on the case so far, promising to contact her if he ever solved the mystery.

After eating a sandwich from a newsagent, he headed off to meet Elena again. Instead of greeting him with a smile as he entered the same coffee shop they had met in for the first time, her face was sullen. She looked up once as he entered, then looked down at a coffee she was languidly stirring.

Slim took a seat opposite, then called the waitress and ordered a coffee.

'Thank you for calling me,' he said. 'I have some updates on your case.'

Elena looked up. 'There's only one thing I want to know, Mr. Hardy. Have you found my mother?'

'No, but—'

Elena lifted a hand, her brow wrinkling. 'Then I don't need to hear more. I received your invoice two days ago, and I of course paid it in full.'

Slim suppressed the urge to grimace. Kim was handling such things now, with an efficiency he had never been able to muster. Had he still been responsible, he would likely never see a penny for his work. Much as he appreciated the payment, he felt a sense of guilt at the lack of positive information he could offer in return.

'I assure you that I'm close to a breakthrough—'

'I'm afraid that I think it's time we closed this investigation,' Elena said, her voice rising as she spoke over him. 'Perhaps it was wishful thinking on my part. I did hope you might have found some answers, though.'

'I'm sorry.'

'It's all right,' she said, her tone telling the truth, that it wasn't, not at all. 'I do thank you for your efforts.'

Elena got up to leave just as Slim's coffee arrived. She gave him a motherly pat on the shoulder as she passed, but she didn't look back.

42

Kᴉᴍ's ᴘʜᴏɴᴇ ᴄᴀʟʟ ᴛʜᴇ ꜰᴏʟʟᴏᴡɪɴɢ ᴍᴏʀɴɪɴɢ confirmed Elena had officially dispensed of his services. Slim, who had spent the night with Lia, wasn't sure how to tell her his business in Holdergate was now over, so after they ate breakfast together he told her he had some paperwork to deal with and headed back to the guesthouse.

His suitcase lay open where he had left it, a pile of laundry recently done in the guesthouse's coin washing machine folded neatly in a plastic bag alongside.

Slim squatted down and started to pack, then changed his mind and stood up. With a staff member in his employ and premises to pay rent on, he no longer had the option of working for nothing. However, it was Tuesday, and it was unlikely Kim could organise a new case before next Monday. He had told the landlady he would stay until the end of the week.

He could at least follow up on the open leads.

Feeling a fresh sense of urgency, he headed for the door.

Charles Bosworth was waiting for him at Holdergate Station. As they boarded a train to Manchester and took seats in the front carriage, Slim's questions were queueing up.

'I feel like I'm being taken on an outing by my grandson,' Bosworth said, beaming out of the window. Then, with a grin, he added, 'A shame we're going no farther than Manchester Piccadilly.'

'I don't want you to feel spoiled,' Slim said.

'I'll pay for the ice-cream,' Bosworth quipped, as he pulled Jennifer's historical case file out of his bag and arranged the papers on his knees.

'I doubted you'd want to keep this casual for long,' he said.

'I have a lead that connects Jennifer to the Peak District Strangler,' Slim said.

Bosworth lifted an eyebrow. 'Do you now?'

'There are a few issues of location and circumstance, but I'm confident she was on his radar.'

He pulled out the same photos he had shown Lia. Bosworth nodded. 'I've seen these before and the resemblance was noted at the time.'

'As we discussed before, it's circumstantial at best,' Slim said. 'The first of the four known Strangler victims wasn't for more than a year afterward, and they were all prostitutes. Their bodies were all found relatively quickly after the murders. Bettelman was working at the time as a delivery driver in Manchester. The blizzard meant there was no way he could have driven to Holdergate on that night. It's not possible, is it?'

Bosworth shook his head. 'No.'

Slim reached into a bag he had brought himself and withdrew two pictures. One was the second picture Toby had given him which showed the man standing by the park fence. The other showed two apparent line sketches of different men's faces.

Kay had faxed Slim the two pictures early that morning. An added note explained how Kay's friend had separated the two composite images as best he could, then filled in the missing information to complete what now appeared like two artists' impressions.

'Do you recognise either of these men?'

'This one, nope, but this one … good God.' Bosworth frowned at the sketch of a man around thirty with a deeply furrowed brow, hard eyes and a savage scar which slashed across the corner of one eye and down to his jawline. Bosworth looked up.

'I want to hear it from you,' Slim said. 'I know what I think, but I want to hear you say it.'

Bosworth let out an airy whistle. 'It's him. That's Jeremy Bettelman, the Peak District Strangler.'

Slim nodded. 'And my next question is how did he happen to be standing at the gate of Holdergate Park when Jennifer Evans came out of the station on the evening of January 15th, 1977?'

43

'THIS IS GENUINE NEW EVIDENCE.' BOSWORTH SAID, barely able to contain his excitement. 'Good God, you really have overturned a few stones. How in the blazes did you find this?'

'Luck, for the most part.'

They had discussed aspects of the case throughout the journey. Slim, however, still had too many holes to fill in before he came to any conclusions. Even proving Bettelman was responsible beyond a reasonable doubt was a hollow result without Jennifer's body. A dead man couldn't reveal a grave's location. There could never be true closure for Elena Trent until her mother was found.

Slim helped Bosworth down from the train and they made their way out to the main concourse. There, they went to an information desk where Slim related the details he had given over the phone that morning. After being asked to wait for a while, they were greeted by a smiling man in overalls.

'Ted Dean,' the man said, offering a hand to both. 'We spoke on the phone. A pleasure to meet you.'

With far more enthusiasm than Slim might have expected of a man who worked among junked trains, Ted Dean led them through a door and out into the goods yard. Slim stared at the rows of rusting locomotives, passenger carriages, and freight wagons lined up across a vast field of sidings tracks that extended nearly as far as the first commuter station at Ashbury.

'She's over here,' Ted said, as Slim, helping Bosworth, who was negotiating the weed-choked rails and pits of rubble and vegetation in between, followed with far less confidence.

'You know,' Ted continued, doubling back to keep his companions in earshot, 'it's so rare that someone shows an interest in one of these old girls, that when you got in touch, I couldn't wait to meet you.'

Bosworth looked ready to flash Ted the badge, but Slim tried to be more convincing with his interest than he had been with Robert Downs. He quoted lines he had memorised from the internet and tried to ask suitably technical questions in order to reinforce his chosen identity of a keen trainspotter.

'Thirty-four years on the Hope Valley, another five running locals on the Manchester metro, then it was retirement for this old girl,' Ted Dean said, reaching up to pat a rusted lump of metal on the corner. 'Well, here she is. I'll leave you and your grandfather alone for a while. Feel free to take a look around. The doors are open so you can go inside. Let me know when you're done. I'll be in the office over there.' He pointed to a corrugated iron shed near the station's back entrance.

Bosworth turned to Slim. 'Grandfather?'

'I suppose I could have been your youngest,' Slim said, grinning.

Bosworth propped up his stick and sat down on a pile of girders while Slim pulled out a digital camera and began taking photographs of the old train. He took a quick look around the outside, then another quick look inside, but most of the internal fittings had been gutted. Finally he turned his attention to the train's underside, squatting down to peer underneath at the wheels and axels and various component parts, taking photographs or at times running his finger over the rusted surfaces, unsure quite what he was looking for, but sure he would know when he saw it. All the while, Bosworth watched him like an old mentor supervising a young protégé.

Finally, after half an hour of stumbling around the old train, Slim packed up his camera and headed back to where the retired policeman sat.

'Thanks for waiting,' he said.

Bosworth smiled. 'I'm sure you'll tell me all about what you found on the way back,' he said.

'Once I'm sure of what I found myself,' Slim said. 'If I found anything at all.'

An hour later, after another long discussion with Ted Dean about things Slim struggled to pretend to understand, he found himself again sitting opposite Bosworth as the train accelerated out of Manchester Piccadilly, a twilight falling over the city behind them.

'So,' Bosworth said, after a few minutes of genial chat. 'I'm guessing you're not a closet trainspotter. What was all that about?'

Slim opened up his camera and turned it around for Bosworth to see. He pointed at a photo of the train's underside.

'I was exploring a possibility,' Slim said. 'It's clear from the original photograph that Jennifer fled from whoever she believed she saw in the snow. We know from the lack of tracks heading elsewhere that she returned to the station. Had she fled back onto the platform, she had to have lost her bag, realistically close enough to the station that it could have found its way to the old bridleway in the jaws of a fox—or, as I believe more likely at this point, a dog—on something sharp or pointed from which it would have taken the amount of power to remove it that stretched the leather around the teeth marks. Are you following?'

Bosworth nodded. 'And you thought she might have tried to duck under the train?'

Slim nodded. 'I was looking for a spot where a woman stooping, perhaps even on her knees, might have had her bag pulled off her shoulder as she fled. And do you know what I found?'

'What?'

'Nowhere.'

Bosworth frowned. 'Which means what?'

Slim stroked his chin. 'My belief at this point is that Jennifer Evans fled back into Holdergate Station and never left.'

44

'Don, I'm afraid I've got another favour to ask.'

Sure,' Donald Lane said. 'What do you have for me?'

'Do you remember a serial killer back in the late seventies called Jeremy Bettelman? He was nicknamed the Peak District Strangler. He killed four women between January and April of 1978, but committed suicide in prison in 1984.'

'Rings a vague bell.'

'I think he's connected in some way to my current case. He was a van driver in the Manchester area. No doubt his movements were investigated. What I'm looking for is a copy of those records. Specifically, I'm looking for the regularity with which he visited Holdergate in the period between December 1977 and the first of his four confirmed murders.'

'Good God, Slim, you don't ask for much.'

'I'm testing you, Don. I want to know just how good you are.'

Don gave a long sigh. 'Give me a couple of days.'

'Thanks, Don.'

Slim hung up, then headed for a lunch date with Lia.

She was waiting in a quiet Italian restaurant just off Holdergate's main square. Slim was surprised to see she had dressed up for the occasion.

She lifted an eyebrow when she took in his appearance. He had shaved, but wore yesterday's jeans and a sweater that was at least three days unwashed.

'I'll give you a chance to remember,' she said, a sly smile on her face. 'Before I chastise you for forgetting what is a quite landmark occasion.'

Slim considered the date. Nothing important popped out. 'Your birthday?' he guessed, although he didn't remember being told.

Lia rolled her eyes then laughed. 'Come on, Slim. How could you possibly forget?' She leaned forward. 'It's our ten-day anniversary. Although,' she added with a smirk and a flick of her right eyebrow he found hopelessly alluring, 'it feels like ten years.'

'Is that a good or bad thing?'

'Depends what time of day it is. You make good scrambled eggs. I've not found a greasy spoon yet that does them better.'

Slim sat down. With a small smile, he said, 'As a matter of fact, I didn't forget.' He reached into his pocket, pulled out his old Nokia. He took a paper napkin out of a holder beside a basket of dressings, wrapped the phone in it and slid it across the table. 'I got you this. It's a vintage model. Collector's item and a family heirloom. Dates to the mid-eighteenth century.'

Lia grinned as she took the phone out of the tissue. 'It's your phone.'

'And my second most valuable possession after my sanity.'

'Which you frequently lose?'

Slim shrugged. 'And find again. Bits of it, at least.'

Lia passed the phone back across. 'I could never accept such a valuable gift. I'll settle for you buying lunch.'

'Done.'

'How's the case going?' Lia asked, after they had ordered.

Slim saw no point lying to her. 'I've been fired,' he said. 'The lady who hired me isn't happy with the progress I've been making. To be fair, I'm not best pleased with it either, but I'm not the one paying for it.'

Lia's face dropped. 'So that means—?'

Slim lifted a hand. 'I'm not leaving, not yet. I'm going rogue, we would say in the army. At least until the end of the week.'

Lia frowned. 'Are you the love-and-leave sort, or is there a point in trying to make something between us work?'

'To be honest, I'm not sure what sort I am.' He gave the back of her hand a squeeze. 'I try to wake up in the same place where I fell asleep and take it from there. But, and I can say this with all honesty, you've come to mean a lot to me. I can't promise I'll be there for you or I won't hurt you, or I won't press a self-destruct button on my life and whatever part of yours is attached to it, because these are things I can't promise to myself. But I can promise that I'll do my best to treat you how you deserve.'

'There's something about you, Slim,' Lia said. 'You're like a box someone has broken open. Most men, they've always got something to hide. They reveal themselves a layer at a time, and it's all fine until you get to a layer you don't like. With you, Slim, I feel like I've already seen the worst.'

'I imagine I could add a few bells and whistles,' he said. 'But if you're prepared to accept the considerable rough, maybe we could make something work.'

Lia's smile was confirmation of her agreement. 'I think the only thing I don't know about you is why people call you Slim.'

'Do you really want to know? Well—'

His phone, lying on the table between them, buzzed. Slim recognised Toby's number.

'I can call him back later,' he said.

'It's fine. It might be important.'

Slim took the phone and answered the call outside the restaurant's entrance. Toby sounded flustered as he said, 'I've been trying to get hold of you for days.'

'I'm sorry. I've been busy catching up on interviews.'

'Have you found anything so far?'

'Nothing I would bet my life on.'

Slim still felt reluctant to open himself up to Toby. The writer brought with him an invisible wall of uncertainty Slim felt disinclined to climb. He appreciated that Toby wanted to help, but was afraid of the other man's unpredictability.

There was one thing, however, that Slim wanted Toby to confirm. He arranged a meeting with the writer for later on that afternoon, recalling as he did a telephone conversation he had had earlier that morning with Denise Layman.

～

'I'm sorry if it feels like I'm cold calling,' Slim said. 'But I'll get straight to the point before you cut me off. I was passed your email by a man named Peter Edwards, whom I believe you went to school with.'

'Oh yes,' Denise said. 'Peter called me yesterday and said to expect your call.'

Slim was glad some of the explaining had been done for him, but nevertheless went over what he had told Peter one more time.

Denise laughed. 'I suppose it's not that often a writer becomes famous enough for people to want to know beyond the books. Toby must have joined an elite club. What in particular would you like to know?'

'Peter told me you were something of a … girlfriend?'

Denise laughed again. 'Oh, nothing like that. I was a bit of a tomboy, and Toby always got on better with girls than boys. Platonically, I mean. He was no ladykiller, but he had the gab. He was the kind of guy you'd ask about what you wanted to wear because you'd get a straight answer.'

Slim frowned. 'Peter told me Toby was untrustworthy.'

'That's because Peter's a man. With girls, Toby was always straight up.'

'Did you go to his house often?'

'Regularly. We'd hang out in his room and look at magazines.'

'His family? What were they like?'

'Nice as pie. His parents doted on him. He used to wind them up something chronic, but they just laughed it off.'

'Did you ever get the impression things weren't what you saw?'

There was a pause on the other end. 'What are you implying, Mr. Hardy?'

'I heard a rumour that his father might have been abusive.'

'Who on Earth did you hear that from?'

'Believe it or not, from Toby himself.'

'That's interesting.' There was another pause. 'Don't forget, you're a man. He might have been trying to impress you.'

'I don't know Toby or his family. I can only go on what I'm told.'

'I know he took medication, and he was absent from school more often than most kids. He'd have a day off at least every couple of weeks. He had endless colds and fevers, but I think that was a side effect of his medicine.'

'What was he taking medicine for?'

'You'd have to ask him, but it was probably for behavioural problems. ADHD, that kind of thing. He never really talked about it, but I'd be at his house and his dad would remind him to take his medicine, which would start an argument. He didn't like it being talked about in front of me. Toby would throw a bit of a tantrum, refuse to take it, which would then escalate into a shouting match until eventually I'd get asked to leave. It was only a couple of times, though. We were friends right up to sixteen. I went off to college, he stayed for A-Levels. Our friend groups changed and we fell out of touch.'

'Interesting,' Slim said. 'Did you never get the impression that there were things going on that you weren't hearing about? Things he might have been in denial about? Repressed things?'

'Never.'

'Did he have siblings?'

'A sister four years younger and an older brother, eight or ten years older, and working by the time I started hanging around Toby. The brother no longer lived with the family, but on the couple of occasions I met him, he was nice enough. And Toby's sister was always cheerful. They argued a lot, but it was nothing unusual. At least not to me.'

∼

Toby's guesthouse stood on the corner of the adjacent road to Slim's. Slim had asked Toby to meet him at the Station Master, and had Lia call him to confirm Toby had arrived. Certain he wouldn't be disturbed, Slim went in through the front entrance of Toby's guesthouse and rang the bell outside the reception counter.

When a lady appeared from an office behind the counter, Slim smiled and introduced himself. 'I'm a friend of Mr. Firth's,' he said. 'I was due to meet him this afternoon, but I got called out on an important appointment. I have something, however, which I'd like to leave for him.'

'I can pass it to him later,' the lady said.

'I'm sure you're busy,' Slim said. 'It's just an envelope. If you tell me his room number I'll slide it under his door.'

'Well, if that's no trouble … it's room six. Second on the left up the stairs.'

'Thanks.'

As the lady indicated a door into the guest hallway and then returned to her office, Slim moved quickly, his old military instincts returning to give him a brief reminder of the man he had once been. He vaulted up the stairs, landing on soft toes to hide the speed of his movement. He had an army-issued lock pick in his hand before he even reached the door, a small metal device which would make short work of an old lock such as these houses had. Pausing to check, however, he found Toby had left the door unlocked, either an oversight or a sign of trust in these quiet little towns.

Inside, Slim quickly established the room's layout, then moved to a bedside cabinet. He opened the second drawer —because no one with anything to hide ever hid it in a top drawer—and got the luck his planning deserved.

Slim carefully lifted a pinch-width of papers to reveal two pill bottles beneath. Without touching them, he pulled a small digital camera from his back pocket, switched it on with one hand, and took a snap with the labels clearly visible.

He replaced the papers exactly as he had found them —a fraction of disturbance might be invisible to the naked eye, but if Toby had taken precautions it would be obvious to a digital camera—and was about to close the drawer when a typed title on the top sheet caught his eye, arousing his curiosity.

It was an article about Tom Jedder. Slim scanned the text, the stylistics identifying it as a historical narrative account, like an encyclopedia entry. However, rather than having the telltale footnotes to indicate a web page downloaded and printed, it had all the formatting marks of something written on a computer.

The first few lines sounded like something he had read online. Had Toby authored it, or just copied it and then reformatted it for printing?

The thud of a closing door downstairs cut off Slim's investigation. He closed the drawer, wiping the handle with a white duster he pulled from a pocket, then returned to the door walking backward, smoothing the scuffs made in the carpet pile by his boot treads as he went. Outside, after closing the door and wiping the handle, he withdrew an envelope from another pocket and slid it under the door as he had promised the landlady. Contained within was a simple apology for missing their appointment and an explanation for not using his phone blamed on messaging glitches.

Finally, to complete the brash, hopeless effect of an aging, alcoholic, disgraced former soldier, he reached into his pocket, withdrew a few pieces of dried dirt he had picked from his boot tread this morning, and scattered them on the ground outside the door in exactly the spot he would have squatted. He dropped a couple more pieces on the stairs for good measure, before thanking the landlady on the way out.

The whole operation had taken less than two minutes.

Then, ignoring the appointment with Toby he still had time to make, he headed for the library to do some more research.

45

Late nights or early mornings were the most interesting times to visit train stations. With the fewest people and the dust of the last or first train still billowing in the empty gap between platforms, the history on display was allowed to plume its feathers, and the ghosts of a million long gone commuters had the space to come out and play.

Of the two, Slim preferred the dawn. He always struggled to get up from a familiar bed, but having been invited to stay over at Lia's, he found himself awake in the pre-dawn shortly after the street lights had switched off. He woke her just enough to excuse himself, then made his way down to Holdergate Station with the night's last stars still shining overhead.

This early, there was no one on duty and the first couple of trains worked on trust, the ticket gates standing open, a box for used tickets next to the ticket counter. No one was waiting for the 0457 to Sheffield, however, so Slim was alone on a deserted platform.

In the pretty but limited town museum he had seen

historical photos of the snowdrifts brought in by that blizzard on that long-ago January day. Dated the 16th, they showed waist-high trenches dug in the piled snow drifts to allow the trains to escape. Slim walked up and down the platform, remembering where the drifts might have been. While much of the front of the station building —the waiting rooms, gift shop, and ticket counter—had been refurbished, the platform area dated back to the 1930s. Aside from a few advertising hoardings promoting local sights and attractions, the platforms looked the same today as they had the day Jennifer stepped off the delayed train and disappeared.

If his theory was right, Jennifer had run back into the station after seeing the man by the park fence, but for some reason had felt no safety among a crowd of people. She had fled back onto the platform, but with no way under the train, she had been presented with two options. Climbing over a drift of snow … or exiting through a gate at the end of the platform which led into the goods yard.

These days, the goods yard was visible through a wire mesh fence, but Slim had seen in historical photographs that it had previously been hidden from view by a tall steel slat fence, which would have also provided shelter from the southerly winds that rattled down out of the hills at night. By the way the snow had drifted in the photos Slim had seen, it would have left a clear space roughly a metre wide along which Jennifer could have run without leaving tracks.

Slim climbed over a low gate and followed the line of the fence, trying to retrace the path Jennifer might have taken. It curved around to end at the buffers for the final pair of rails in the goods yard. This last section of track now held three decrepit box cars, much of the wood walls rotted to nothing, leaving only the metal wheels and the frames. Beyond them, the fence reached an overgrown corner and headed back to end at the main line tracks. Backed up in the corner was the small, tumbledown shed Slim had noticed from the window of the Station Master.

He picked his way towards it through the grass, brambles and weeds, catching his feet on buried pieces of machinery, the remains of another abandoned siding track now rusted to the colour of earth, and a lump of protruding concrete where buffers had once been embedded.

The shed's door was long gone, the roof so collapsed Slim had to duck down to peer inside. He pulled a torch from his pocket and waved it around, revealing only corrugated iron and brambles. What dimensions the shed might have once had were impossible to see.

Getting on to his hands and knees, he started to crawl forward, pausing when his jacket sleeve caught on a metal peg halfway up the door frame. He guessed from its height that it had once been used to hook the door shut. Frustrated, he turned to tug his jacket free and felt a sudden shiver of cold as though a gust of wind had blown down his neck.

Careful not to touch it with his hand, he used the already damaged section of coat to twist the peg free from its rusted fitting before dropping it into his pocket.

Had Jennifer reached the end of her own line in this tiny shed in the back corner of Holdergate's goods yard? It had the feel of a last chance saloon. Here, Jennifer would have found herself cornered, unable to go any farther without leaving a trail.

But why?

What would have made her so afraid of the man she

saw that she couldn't trust to her safety in a crowd numbering several hundred?

Slim shook his head and gave a brief shrug, then turned and made his way out of the goods yard before the first arriving workers could discover him.

46

'I WAS JUST ABOUT TO CALL YOU,' DON SAID. 'BELIEVE IT or not, I managed to dig out what you asked for. Don't ask me where I got it or I'll double the fee for your next request. If you give me a fax number I can send it through right away.'

Slim gave Don the fax for the local post office where he had arranged to pick up messages. 'And about that extra request ... I'd like you to dig up a list of employees from Holdergate Station in 1977.'

Don gave a short laugh. 'Easy after that last one. I'll be in touch again in a day or two.'

Slim hung up, then headed down to the post office.

True to his word, Don had come up with the goods. Faxed were ten photocopied pages of old ledgers from a transportation company, complete with driver names, dates, goods being transited, and the destination address.

Slim took the faxed documents up to the library, where he photocopied a local regional map and spent a couple of hours drawing pencil lines from the company offices in

Manchester to locations including Sheffield, Stockport and Huddersfield, each assigned to Jeremy Bettelman.

Between the dates of December 1977 and January 1979, Bettelman had undertaken more than fifty assignments to locations that required him to cross the Peak District. There were few decent roads and on any occasion he could have taken a route that took him through Holdergate.

On more than a dozen occasions, a comment had been added in an extra column stating something to do with a delay. Five occasions mentioned lateness due to getting lost en route, three more mentioned mechanical problems, and another couple simply said LATE DELIVERY.

Interestingly, a line drawn in black felt-tip, one Slim assumed had been added by a police officer during the investigation, marked an abrupt shift in the locations from distant towns and villages requiring a couple of hours' drive, to mostly Manchester metropolitan area-based. A circled note said that at this point Bettelman had become a full-time employee. Following this were four starred entries with other police-added notes claiming them as the likely disposal dates for the four murder victims.

Slim gave a slow nod. 'You knew when your schedule would take you back up there, didn't you?' he muttered. 'You killed them, and then you took them up into the hills to dump. But what were you doing up there before then?'

There could only be one possible reason. Slim folded up the map and headed out.

47

ELENA LOOKED UNCOMFORTABLE TO FIND SLIM STANDING on her doorstep. He was aware he hadn't shaved in a couple of days nor changed his clothes, but he had stayed off the drink. Things could be worse.

'I'm not sure to what I owe this social call—'

'I'm sorry to drop by unexpectedly like this, but I wanted to let you know that I'm not done with your case,' Slim said. 'You might be, but I'm not. I'm no longer working for you, however. I'm doing this for myself. I have a couple of questions. I can ask them here, or I can ask them inside. That would be preferable.'

With a tired shrug, Elena said, 'Then I guess you'd better come in.'

She led him through into a small but pretty living room, decked out in floral patterns and motifs. A fresh bunch of flowers sat in a vase on a corner table, and the room was well lit from a bay window facing east. Slim took a seat on a two-seater sofa and pulled a file out of his bag.

'I'd prefer it if you sat down,' Slim said as Elena lingered in the doorway, fidgeting with her hands. 'I want to show you a couple of photographs and I'd like to see your reaction.'

'Photographs of what?'

'Please sit down.'

Somewhat reluctantly Elena perched herself on the edge of an armchair, hands placed neatly in her lap. Slim withdrew a photograph and held it out.

'Have you ever seen this man?'

Elena leaned forward, frowning. After a few seconds she shook her head. 'No ... not that I recall.'

'That's fine. How about this one?'

Slim pulled the first photograph quickly away to reveal a nearly identical picture directly beneath. Elena's reaction was instantaneous. She let out a little gasp then drew back, hands over her mouth.

'You've seen him, haven't you? Tell me where.'

Elena buried her face in her hands. 'He was watching me ... oh Lord, he was watching me.'

Slim looked at the pictures again. They showed two very similar men's faces, both in their early twenties, but one with a naturally sneering look and a vicious scar that ran down his face from the bottom of his right eye to his jawline.

Jim Randall and Jeremy Bettelman, two brothers, one with an almost cherubic innocence, the other carrying the eyes and appearance of a devil in human skin. The police photograph that would make Bettelman famous had of course been taken two years later, when he was wearing a full beard with only the first inch of the scar visible above it. This picture could be the face of a different man, and Elena's reaction, despite how distressed she had become, was the one Slim had been hoping for.

'You saw him watching your house, didn't you?'

Elena, still covering her mouth, gave a frantic nod. 'Yes, yes, I did. On three separate occasions. The first time he was idling across the street when I came home from school. I didn't think much of it because I'd never seen him before, but I immediately noticed that scar. The other two were at night. Once was near my school. The other in the park across the street. He was sitting on a bench, looking across at our house.'

'When would this have been?'

Elena shrugged, shaking her head. 'Oh, I'd guess the summer and autumn of 1977. It was after my mother had disappeared because I remember feeling isolated, unprotected. My dad was still struggling to hold a job, so often wouldn't be home until long after I'd got back from school. The three occasions were spaced out, and I would have just about put the previous time out of my mind when I saw him again. The last one could have been October or November, because it was dark, but I remember it was not that late.'

'And do you know the identity of this man?'

Elena shook her head. 'I'm sorry, I don't. After I stopped seeing him I gradually forgot about him. I figured it was just coincidence, that he was a local perhaps, who had moved away.'

Slim pulled out a mugshot of the bearded Bettelman after his arrest. 'The Strangler,' he said. 'He was the Peak District Strangler.'

Elena let out another little gasp. 'Oh my. He was after me?'

Slim shook his head. 'Not you,' he said. 'I believe he had no interest in you at all, and that you kept seeing him was just bad luck. I believe he was after your mother. He was after Jennifer.'

48

'I DON'T HAVE ABSOLUTE PROOF,' SLIM SAID, SIPPING A coffee as he sat across from Lia. 'But I'm close. If I can only find her, I'm sure I'll be able to prove it.'

'She wasn't a victim of the Strangler?'

Slim shook his head. 'No. But she was meant to be. My theory is that she befriended Jim Randall in hospital, and provided him with something which would end his pain. But either some time before he died or on his deathbed, he revealed her identity to his brother. Incensed, Jeremy went after her.'

'But how did he end up in Holdergate? He was a delivery driver. No way could he have driven up here through that snow.'

'He didn't. I spoke to my contact in Manchester, a man who knew both brothers. Bettelman was only working part-time for the delivery company at that time. At night he was moonlighting, working cash in hand in a loader's yard.'

'Where?'

'Outside Manchester Piccadilly. Robert told me a freight train came in just after the commuter Jennifer was on. Jeremy was on it, stowed away. He must have been as surprised as her that the snow stopped them at Holdergate. The freight was diverted out to a wide siding track, and Jeremy, perhaps afraid of being discovered, climbed over the fence, went around and approached the station from the front.'

'And Jennifer saw him watching her?'

'Yes. But—and here's where I'm guessing a little—Jennifer didn't know about Jim's brother. I talked to Elena, who told me her mother was deeply religious. Church every Sunday, prayers before meals. It must have gone against every one of her core values to help Jim die. Therefore, when she sees a scarred, angry older version watching her, what's she going to think?'

Lia leaned back in her chair. 'The devil. She thought the devil had come after her.'

'Exactly. It would literally have put the fear of God into her, and she might have felt that even a station full of people would be no protection. In a blind panic she runs right through, back out onto the platform. She's trying not to leave tracks to be followed, but there's snow everywhere. The only way she could see free of snow is a path out into the goods yard.'

'She got away?'

'Initially. My guess is Bettelman panicked at the sight of so many people and did a runner, perhaps back to the train, perhaps hiding out overnight. But he came back, over and over again across the following year, whenever he could get away with it on his schedule without it being too obvious. He was hunting her. Eventually he must have realised she had disappeared, or perhaps seen something in the newspaper. Still incensed, he began to look for somewhere else to take out his anger. He encountered Jim's old girlfriend, and began killing prostitutes.'

'So what happened to Jennifer if Bettelman didn't kill her?'

'Someone else did.'

'Who?'

'Tom Jedder.'

'And who on earth is that?'

Slim spread his hands and smiled. 'At this point, I have no idea.'

49

DELUSION. DEPRESSION. PSYCHOSIS. IRRATIONALITY. The list of Toby's symptoms went on and on. What the two bottles of medication didn't answer were why. What had caused Toby's illness, however it was described, and what effect, if any, did it have on Jennifer's case?

Slim was still mulling over these things when the cafe's door opened and Toby entered. Slim stood up quickly, offering a hand and an apology for missing their previous meeting.

'I'm so sorry, I double-booked you with someone else,' he said, feeling a brief stab of guilt at the lie. 'I was halfway to Manchester before I realised.'

Toby shrugged and took a seat across the table. 'Quite all right. These things happen. I gather the case is coming along well?'

Slim smiled. 'In some ways. I'm not getting far with any answers, but I've been figuring out a lot of the things which didn't happen.'

'Such as?'

'She wasn't a victim of the Strangler. Jeremy Bettelman

had an alibi for that day.' Slim felt that now was not the time to reveal who he had identified as the man in Toby's photograph. 'I have a couple of questions to ask you, though. Some things I'd like to clarify.'

'Sure, go ahead.'

Slim took two pictures out of a folder and passed them across. One was the drawing of the man identified in the reflection. The other the picture of Jim Randall after being put through a sketch converter on an online paint program.

'Was either of these men the one you saw that night outside Holdergate Park?'

Toby frowned then shook his head. He pointed at the picture of the reflected man and said, 'This one looks familiar. This other, though … I have no idea.'

Slim sat back, being careful to hide his disappointment. He had hoped Toby would identify the reflected man as his own father, whom Slim suspected it to be. Perhaps the drawing's likeness wasn't close enough.

'If you remember, please let me know.'

'Of course.'

A minute of awkward silence passed between them. Slim had something else to ask but wasn't sure how to bring it up. In the end, Toby got in first, pulling a scruffy handful of papers out of his bag.

'I found some more information I thought might interest you,' he said. 'It's about Tom Jedder.'

Slim looked down at the printed web pages and read the first few lines. Barring the odd grammatical correction, it was word for word what he had read on the prints he had seen in Toby's drawer.

'Where did you get these?' he said. 'I couldn't find

anything other than a brief reference in a history book to a local mine worker of that name.'

Toby grinned. 'You have to know where to look. I'd guess as a writer I've spent a lot more time researching things on the internet than you have.'

Slim doubted it, but he appeased Toby with a nod and a smile. Let the man think he was played. 'Can I take these to read over?'

'Sure. These are copies I made for you. I can summarise them briefly if you like.' Without Slim responding either way, Toby continued, 'Jedder disappeared without a trace in around 1930. It was believed some sort of accident had befallen him, or perhaps he had even been murdered. A few years later, he began to be seen again, around the anniversary of his death.' Toby leaned forward. 'Get this. While you might expect to see a ghostly representation of a boy, Jedder appeared to be aging. Not as fast as you or I, but gradually, a year for every three or four of ours. He was aging, but something else was happening. He was fading, too. His features were starting to disappear. His eyes were closing up, his nose and mouth shrinking. Something like this.'

Toby thrust a picture across the table. It was a drawing of some kind of horror movie character, a man with tiny facial features, receding hair, slumped ears, no noticeable chin.

'What the hell is this?' Slim said, pushing it away in revulsion.

Toby pulled out another picture, this one a print of the Polaroid he had taken but withheld from the police.

'It's an artist's impression of the Visitor I saw that night. It's quite clear that's what he was, and whatever dimension he went to was slowly taking his humanity away from this one.'

Slim looked up, his anger rising. 'Look, I've had just about enough of this crap.' He jabbed a finger at the photograph, at the man standing outside the fence. 'It's a damn reflection, and I can prove it—'

Toby sat up. His eyes twinkled as he shook his head, a grin that hinted at madness spreading across his face. 'Oh, not *him*. I'm not talking about him, Mr. Hardy. I'm talking about *the other man*, the one peering through the railings in the fence.'

As Toby's finger snaked out, indicating a tiny white circle Slim had thought was a snowflake glare on the camera lens but was in fact the outline of a face pressed between two fence railings, he felt an uncontrollable urge to punch the triumphant smirk off Toby's face. Instead, realising with sudden horrifying clarity the aberration which may have been the root cause of Toby's lifetime of mental illness, he slipped from his chair and went crashing to the floor.

50

'IT'S IMPOSSIBLE TO SEE WHAT IT IS,' LIA SAID. 'HE SAID it's a face, but it could be anything. A bulge in the film, a reflection. You can't trust a word he's telling you.'

Slim nodded. 'I sent it back to my friend in linguistics, and he passed it on to the specialist who decoded the two people in that picture. He didn't even notice it. Even with Toby's claim, there's no proof it's a face.'

'He's a novelist, and he's crazy,' Lia said. 'I imagine the two complement each other pretty well.'

Slim took a sip of his coffee. 'I'm convinced at this point that Toby's playing me for a mug. I asked another friend to get me some info on these sites he's supposedly pulling these documents from, and he couldn't find anything. Said if there's anything on the web it's encrypted, on a private server, but what he suspected was more likely was that the prints were formatted on a computer to look like web printouts. He thinks Toby wrote them himself, which is what I think now, too.'

'Why?'

'I think that he truly believes he saw something

terrifying that night. You have to remember, he was a six-year-old kid, playing with his first camera, seeing that kind of snow for the first time. He was living a fantasy already. And then there's the fact that for one reason or another he might have been the last person to see Jennifer Evans alive. He knew that, because police questioned him. It's in the reports. This is a little kid, and he thought he saw something out there, and over time it's manifested in his mind to something infinitely terrifying. He started having psychotic episodes, leading to a dependency on medication and strange personality traits which included the craving of attention and excessive deceit as a way of gaining it. And then, as an adult, he learned how to channel it into his writing.'

Lia rubbed her chin. 'Didn't you say your secretary read his books? Perhaps you should ask her if there are any elements of this which tie up with what Toby's been telling you.'

Slim nodded. 'I'll call her this afternoon.' He pulled the folder of notes he had made out of his bag. 'In the meantime, could you do me a favour?' He pointed at the second picture he had shown Toby, the one he had been convinced was Toby's father. 'Could you show this picture to your mother? I need to know who this was. It could be significant, or it could mean nothing at all. If she lived in Holdergate back then she might recognise him. It could be a local, and if so, I'd really like to know what they saw.'

Lia nodded. 'Sure.' She started to get up, then reached across and squeezed Slim's hand. 'I had a thought. It sounds stupid, but what if … what if Jennifer also saw the other person?'

Slim shook his head. 'I'm thinking that Toby's out of his mind, that's all. I can't believe that's actually a face.'

'But let's say he isn't the complete nutjob he appears to be, and he really did see something else he thought was a face. If Jennifer saw it, and it looked anything like that monster in the picture you showed me … it would have scared a God-fearing girl like Jennifer like nothing else could.'

'Why?'

'Jezebel.'

'Who?'

'The fallen angel. Satan's very own sidekick.'

Slim frowned. 'What?'

'I've got to run,' Lia said. 'I'll explain it later.'

Slim watched her go, then finished up his coffee and headed out.

51

'I'M SO SORRY TO BOTHER YOU,' SLIM SAID AS THERESA opened the door. 'I wondered if Robert was home. I meant to call ahead but my phone battery died.'

For once, it wasn't an excuse. His phone had given up the ghost halfway through a call to Kim. Slim had thought about heading back to the guesthouse to recharge it, but he was already halfway to Robert's house and figured he could at least see if the old guy was home.

Theresa shook her head. 'I'm afraid he's not here right now, but if you want to come in a moment, I'll check his diary to see when he'll be back.'

The old lady led Slim into a quiet living room. A comfortable armchair sat beside a recliner, both angled toward a large TV. A towering bookshelf stood against one wall, overloaded with books which at a glance followed a railways or Peak District theme. Beside it was a cluttered dresser adorned with photographs and ornaments. Theresa left Slim standing beside it while she went through into a kitchen. Slim looked around him, taking in the comforts of late middle-age, admiring the collection of books which must have cost a fortune, then casting his eyes over dozens of framed photographs, some of them black and white, dating back perhaps fifty years. In a large, ornate-framed one placed centrally, a silver-haired couple smiled as they cut a wedding cake.

Theresa returned, holding a Filofax open. 'I'm afraid he's gone to bridge club. I thought that was Wednesday, but apparently Wednesday is the local wildlife committee … in any case, he won't likely be back until later this afternoon.'

'It's okay,' Slim said. 'Could you tell him I stopped by? I just had a few more questions. Nothing too urgent.'

'Certainly. I'll let him know.'

As he turned to leave, Slim nodded at the wedding photo. 'I thought Robert said you weren't married?'

The woman laughed. 'We're not, legally. We had a mock ceremony, but that was all. Robert didn't want to do it all again.'

'He was married before?'

'Oh yes, but a long time ago now. She died young, though. He never really talks about her, but if I'm honest, I don't want to know. I know she's long dead, but she's still my competition, isn't she?'

Slim smiled. He wondered if Lia would ever think that about his ex-wife, then found himself almost bursting into laughter. 'Don't worry, I'll keep it to myself,' he said. 'So you're not from round here?'

'Oh no. I'm from Suffolk, way down south. We met on holiday.'

She looked about to open the floodgates about their history, so Slim made his excuses and left. He returned to the guesthouse, left his phone on charge, and then went to the library.

Jezebel. According to the Old Testament, she had been Ahab's queen. Turned on by her supporters for persecuting Christians, she had been thrown from a window, then had her flesh eaten by dogs. She was often depicted in literature as a fallen angel, while her use of cosmetics had linked makeup and gaudiness to prostitution.

Lia was right. Had Jennifer seen Bettelman and considered him the devil, the presence of some other, monstrous person linked to a persecuted biblical figure might have driven her close to madness.

But who had it been?

52

IT SOMETIMES FELT EASIER TO ASSUME HIS GUISE AS Mike Lewis, BBC documentary researcher, than it did to maintain his regular persona. Sometimes, even Lewis had to do the dirty work, Slim thought, as he went door to door around Holdergate, showing copies of Toby's horror caricature to residents under the pretext of researching an urban legend from the seventies and eighties.

After a couple of dozen houses, during which he was met with repulsed looks and a few harsh words but no information, he began to feel the old pull, the draw back to his own sense of oblivion. The lights of local pubs seemed brighter than those of other establishments, and the booze racks of newsagents seemed to have little voices infiltrating his thoughts.

He had ironically monikered the faceless man as "Facey", but no one he spoke to knew anything. With his feet beginning to drag, and his fingers to shake from a need he was struggling to control, he knocked on one more door, steeling himself for the same spiel he had divulged time and time again until the words felt hollow in his mouth like an old piece of gum he couldn't find somewhere to throw away. He waited on the step for the door to open, introduced himself with feigned enthusiasm, explained himself and held up the drawing.

Minutes later, weary beyond words, he stumbled across the street, through an overgrown gateway into a small neglected park which bordered the train line. He brushed brambles off a bench and pulled out his phone.

Lia answered on the second ring.

'Help me.'

'Slim? Where are you?'

He looked around him. 'Near the tracks. I'm not sure. A park. There's a pub nearby called The Apple Tree. I need to drink. Help me, Lia.'

His voice cracked even as he said it, both sorrowful for using her as a crutch but in a way also relieved that he had leaned on her before he leaned on the booze. He would break her eventually and they both knew it, but for now she was holding him up.

'I'm at work, Slim....'

'I know. I just ... I didn't know what else to do.'

'It's okay. Hang on, I'll sneak out the back. We're not busy. Don't move. Don't ring off. I'm five minutes away, that's all.'

The shakes were right up to his elbows now, not so much from the dependency he had broken a dozen times but from the memory of it.

He waited. The seconds beat in his ears like the wings of bats, hammering the side of his face. He got up, waiting for the temptation to pass, but it persisted, claws holding on to his shoulders. The pub was a few doors up the nearest street, an OPEN sign outside. A hundred-metre walk. It would only take one drink to settle him. Perhaps if he had just one, a half maybe, to steady him, to make the shaking ease, he could get back out on the job. Just a half. That's all he needed.

He turned for the way he had come in, but it was no longer there. A hedgerow rose up in front of him, blocking the way forward. Butterflies made his vision flicker, and a high-pitched wail blocked out all other sound. The ground rumbled, something terrible approaching, and Slim threw himself at the hedgerow, determined to get away. Brambles, hawthorn, and nettles slashed at his face, stinging and scratching him. He ripped them aside, bloodying his hands. He dug his way forward until he was nearly face down, his feet caught, a broken branch digging into his stomach, and then something massive rushed past on the other side of the hedge.

He screamed. The roar of engines rose to meet it, then they were receding, leaving only the lingering ring of his voice behind.

'Slim?'

He opened his eyes. All movement had stopped except the thundering of his heart and the gravelly intake of his breath. The train had hurried on down the line, leaving only the humming of the rails in its wake.

'Slim? Are you all right?'

The craving had gone. Slim pushed himself backward until he landed in a bloody, scuffed heap in the long grass at the hedge's foot. Lia stood over him, eyes wide. A hand reached down to help him up, and he pulled her forward into an embrace, aware he had begun to cry.

'Thank you,' he whispered. 'Thank you for coming.'

'What were you doing? You could have fallen onto the line.'

Slim looked around him. In his disorientation he had

got turned around. Instead of heading for the street he had tried to climb over the thick, overgrown hedgerow separating the park from the railway line. He had left a ragged swathe through the undergrowth, and it had left its mark on him in a series of harsh scratches on his arms and an area of nettle rash on his stomach where the hawthorn branches had pulled up his sweater.

'Something happened.' He shook his head, trying to remember the exact reason for his sudden panic attack. It came back with a jolt, like a hard slap to the face.

The crumpled sheet of paper lay on the grass nearby. Slim picked it up, reluctantly turning it over to reveal Facey on the other side.

'Someone remembered him,' Slim said, shivering. 'Someone remembered Facey.'

53

THEY WENT FOR COFFEE. SLIM'S HANDS SHOOK AS HE drank, but no longer through a craving for drink, only out of fear. The look in the old woman's eyes as they filled with tears. One hand rubbed her nose, then she ducked her head, unable to meet Slim's eyes.

'Oh, I remember him,' she said. 'Poor tragic thing.'

She had few details to elaborate with, nor did she recall his name.

'No one local ever liked to stand at the far eastern end of the platform,' she told Slim, her eyes downcast as though recalling the way she might once have been while waiting for a train. 'You could see into the goods yard from there, and sometimes he'd be about. Not often, just once in a while. And always playing with that dog of his, the pair of them clambering among the junk and the old trains.'

Tom Jedder. The monster Slim had christened Facey had to be Tom Jedder, Toby's Visitor, his ghost.

Except that he wasn't an aberration from a fantasy novel, but a very real person.

Lia had to go back to work. Slim gave her a fierce hug,

promising to call her if he felt himself sliding again. He wanted to say more, perhaps to offer her three words he hadn't said to anyone in decades, but even after she had stepped up for him, put herself on the line for a man she still barely knew, he was afraid. Was he confusing dependency for something more? And if he wasn't, did he want to burden her with something so heavy, something that would perhaps make it even harder for her to walk away?

Resuming his search for information, now armed with what the old lady had told him, it wasn't long before he found others who dredged nightmares from the depths of their memories. An elderly gentleman who had once worked in an office near the station recalled seeing Facey playing in the park one evening, long after it was usually deserted. Walking past on his way home, he had come upon the figure by surprise, and caught just a glimpse before Facey bolted, pursued by a little white dog.

Another elderly lady remembered seeing a short, nearly bald figure running among the siding tracks in the goods yard at Holdergate Station late one night while waiting for a delayed train to Manchester.

'From the moment I caught a glimpse of that face I tried to forget it,' the lady said. 'A trick of the light, car lights catching something reflective through the slats in the fence. I only saw it for an instant, and always tried to put it out of my mind. And until I saw that picture of yours, I thought I had.'

Yet still no connection to Tom Jedder beyond what Toby claimed, and what old Litchfield had said. Slim wanted to visit the old man again, but worried the picture might be too much of a shock for him.

Instead, he turned his attention back to Toby. Back at

the guesthouse, he lay on the bed and called Kim, catching her just before she left the office.

After giving her an update on what had happened over the last few days, he told her what he had learned about Jedder, Facey, and the dog, and asked her if she had seen any parallels in Toby's novels.

'Well,' she said. 'Since you mention it, there was something. Don't go on what I say, but check the online reviews for the fourth book. They're scathing. There's a sequence in the book where one of the minor villains—a shapeshifter called No-Face—dies in a particularly gruesome manner. He is tied across a train track and gets decapitated. You might expect that sort of thing in a book for adults, but this is a children's book, remember. Fans were up in arms, apparently, parents asking for the passage to be removed. According to a gossip website, the third book undersold and the publisher allowed that passage to remain in order to generate a bit of publicity.'

'Did you check it out?'

Kim laughed. 'Of course. I called the publisher, but got "no comment". They wouldn't talk to me.'

'What are the circumstances around it?'

'Well, it's actually carried out by the main character, and when No-Face dies, it releases the main character from a negativity curse. You know, in the context of the story, it works, but it could have been done a little less violently, in my opinion, considering the audience.'

'That's interesting. Anything else?'

'Well, I don't know if it's important, but No-Face appears from a dream the character has. At the beginning he's a normal boy, but he gradually starts to change into a monster. Do you think it could be autobiographical? That Tobin P. Firth killed this person you're looking for?'

Slim shook his head. 'I haven't ruled it out,' he said. 'I think it's unlikely. It's more likely a form of catharsis. There's a character Toby has in his head which is haunting him. I believe he knew about the person's death and wrote it into his book as a way of expressing his own closure.'

'Well, I guess it's possible.'

Slim nodded. 'Thanks, Kim. Your information was a great help.'

It was still light outside, and Slim felt restless. He went out, walking the streets until he found himself at the bottom of Charles Bosworth's road. A light was on in the old policeman's living room, so Slim went up to the door and knocked.

Bosworth appeared pleased to see him and invited him inside.

'How's the case going?' he asked, offering Slim a seat and his choice of drinks. Back in control after the earlier episode, Slim opted for tonic water on ice, claiming he was still on duty.

'I've made some progress,' he said. 'I don't know what it'll lead to as I still haven't come up with a body.'

'But you have some new leads since we last spoke?'

Slim shrugged. 'Maybe. Something I wanted to ask you … you were still working for Derbyshire Constabulary through the eighties, weren't you?'

Bosworth nodded. 'I retired in 1996.'

'So you dealt with your share of train suicides? Or would that be the jurisdiction of the transport police?'

'We'd pick them up and phone them in. So yeah, I dealt with a few.' He gave a deep frown. 'Never a pleasant experience.'

Slim pulled Facey's picture out of his back pocket and slid it across the table.

'Was this person ever one of them?'

At the sight of Facey, Bosworth immediately winced, leaving Slim no doubt he had seen the person before.

'Oh, Slim, where did you get this?'

'I'll keep that to myself for the time being, if you don't mind.'

Bosworth nodded. 'Said like a true policeman. Yes, I've seen this person before, although the likeness isn't exact. He died on the train line in September 1982.'

'Was he decapitated?'

Bosworth closed his eyes for a long time. 'How do you figure these things out? Yes, and no. He was, but perhaps not the way you think. He was struck from behind. The train's driver testified that the figure appeared to be kneeling on the tracks at the time, his head lowered, facing away from the train. The spot at which he was struck was on a slight bend where the verges had a propensity to become overgrown late in the year. The driver had no chance to stop. He blew the train's horn as is protocol, but the figure didn't move.'

'And who was he?'

'A most unfortunate local boy. I'm afraid I couldn't tell you much more. He was Holdergate's unwanted secret.'

'How do you mean?'

'I saw him alive only once, a year or so before then. I was on a train, coming into Holdergate Station. The boy was walking along the tracks. He glanced up as we passed, and the sight of him was enough to send a shiver through my heart.'

'Was he known around the town?'

'You didn't speak of him. Yes, some local people knew of his existence, but you wouldn't acknowledge him openly, and you wouldn't talk about him.'

'That's … heartless.'

'It makes me ashamed to think of it, even now. It wasn't intentional. That he was so rarely seen made it worse, because you'd build up an image of him in your mind until it was almost like a shadow that would follow you home.'

'It's a horrible way to treat someone.'

Bosworth sighed. 'I remember a former colleague saying he would flinch at the yapping of any small dog, for fear it was that boy nearby.'

'He had a dog?'

'Yes, a small white terrier thing. A Scottsdale, maybe.'

Slim frowned. For a few seconds he racked his brain, certain he had seen such a dog somewhere before, wishing his memory hadn't been softened by years of alcohol abuse. 'He had a dog of the right size that could have left the marks in Jennifer's bag?'

'Well, I guess it would have fit.'

Slim leaned forward. 'And you didn't add all this up back in 1977? It's my belief that the person in this picture was responsible for Jennifer's disappearance. I believe she encountered him on that night, and was likely murdered.'

Bosworth gave a tired laugh. 'A fanciful idea, Slim, but one that's astray, I'm afraid.'

'Why?'

'Because the boy in this picture was just nine at the time of his death. At the time of Jennifer's disappearance, therefore, he would have been just four years old. Even in this day and age, not many four-year-olds commit first-degree murder, do they?'

54

SLIM SPREAD THE PRINTS AND SCRIBBLED SHEETS OUT ON his bed. Saturday night. He was leaving first thing Sunday morning, but did he have enough to close the mystery down? He was close, so close, but the one thing he so desperately needed still eluded him.

Jennifer's body.

If he found her remains, he could make the evidence he had found stick.

Where was she?

Bosworth had claimed not to recall the name of the boy Slim called Facey, and the case file had been lost over the years. A little too conveniently, Slim thought.

He looked at the prints Don had sent him, then reached for the bottle of whisky beside his bed.

'I'm sorry, Lia,' he whispered, glad she wasn't here to see him fall off the wagon once again, but the girl had done her part. He recalled their brief phone conversation earlier that afternoon:

'Slim, I spoke to my mother. She recognised the man in that picture.'

It made perfect sense. And this morning he had gone back to visit Litchfield in the retirement home. Instead of getting to the questions he wanted to ask, Slim had just sat and listened to the old man, noticing the slur in his voice, the way certain letters blurred into each other, a lisp perhaps evident from childhood which might have turned certain words into others. Words which might have passed from one person to another, until the original meaning was lost, and a new meaning had taken its place.

Don had come up with the goods, and Kay had done his part, too. Shoveling everything he had collected into a plastic bag, Slim took one last swig of the whisky and went out.

He had to start shouting before lights came on and someone appeared behind the frosted glass in the doorway.

'Let me in, damn you,' Slim shouted. 'Let me in or I'll tell the whole street what you did to Jennifer Evans.'

The door opened, revealing a figure in a dressing gown. Slim glared at him, breathing hard from the long uphill walk, glad he had stuffed the whisky back into his jacket beforehand. He held up the crumpled picture of Facey.

'No more questions. I want answers.'

The figure in the dressing gown gave a long, deflating sigh and nodded.

'You'd better come in,' Robert Downs said.

55

'YOU'D NEED MORE EVIDENCE,' KAY SAID. 'HOWEVER, you're right. My contact found traces of leather on that peg. There's no proof it came from a bag strap—at least not without the bag in question being available for analysis—but there's a pretty good chance, don't you think?'

With a distressed Theresa banished upstairs, her threats to call the police quelled by a few calming words from Robert, Slim faced Holdergate's former station master across the room, a collection of crumpled prints in his hands brandished like weapons.

'You can be straight and tell me what happened, or I can present my findings to the police, and we'll see how you fare under official interrogation,' Slim said, playing his prosecution threat card early, hoping Robert fell for it rather than questioned the depth of Slim's evidence. Such bullying tactics against an old and gentle man left a sour taste on his tongue, but Slim remembered he was facing a probable murderer.

'You were alone there that night,' Slim said. 'I had a friend dig out an old staff roster, and after seven p.m. the station had only one man on duty. That's what caused so much trouble. You were dealing with a station full of people without assistance, and when you realized someone had seen your boy, you panicked.'

'My boy....' Robert wiped away a tear. 'Can't you please leave him out of this?'

'Not when he's the center of everything.'

Robert slumped into his recliner. Behind him, on the dresser shelf, Slim saw again the photograph he'd barely registered last time: no more than five centimetres high, it sat nearly tucked away behind the large, colourful wedding photo.

A view from behind of a boy kneeling down, hugging a little white dog against his knees.

'Your son, Thomas Edward Downs.'

Robert sniffed. 'I loved that boy like nothing else in the world. I was the only one who did, but even I couldn't bear to photograph his face. It was as though if I couldn't see it, I could imagine it the way I wanted it to be.'

'He was born in 1973,' Slim said, pushing across a photocopy of a birth certificate Don had obtained for him. And your wife, Julie, died in December 1974. Suicide by hanging.'

Robert closed his eyes as tears streamed down his face. 'Why do you have to bring all this up?'

'She couldn't deal with a child with Thomas's deformities.'

Robert sighed and nodded, holding his head in his hands. 'She wanted him sent away to a special home, but I refused. It was the shame killed her in the end, the neighbours' glances, the words she'd not quite overhear. After she was gone, I kept the boy with me all the time, because he wasn't just my boy, but my link to her.'

Slim nodded. 'While you were working, you hid him in that shed in the goods yard, by the fence, didn't you? I managed to get in contact with a couple of your younger colleagues. They told me no one was allowed in that shed, and when you were off duty it was kept padlocked. Only you had a key.'

Robert nodded. 'I put a heater and a light in there, and filled it with toys and magazines. He would never stay put, though. He was always wandering around the goods yard. That boy loved two things in life, the little dog I bought him and trains. He later started wandering up and down the line while I was working. That was when he died. His little dog had passed away the day before. The last time I ever saw him he was carrying a box across the goods yard toward the main line. I think he carried it along a way to a pretty place, then left its body on the tracks. Some kind of ritual of his own devising.'

Slim wished he had more to drink. 'Tell me about the night of the blizzard. A friend's mother recognised your picture. You saw the boy taking the photograph. And if you were close enough, it's my belief you saw Jennifer, too.'

Robert massaged his brow. 'It breaks my heart to think it, but no one would have run like that unless they saw my boy.'

'What was he doing in the park? That's where I believe he was that night.'

'He was still a little boy, despite everything. While I was working the late shift, I would take his dinner out to the shed, but once he was done he would sneak out, climb over the wall and go up to the park when it was deserted and he could play by himself. And that night it was snowing, of course.' Robert sighed again. 'Because of the blizzard, I told him to stay in the shed where I knew he'd be safe, so when I saw her run through the station in the direction of the platforms, I went to check.'

'You followed her?'

Robert gave half a shrug. 'I wondered where she had gone, but she wasn't my concern. By the time I made it to the platform she was nowhere to be seen. I did wonder if she'd got back on the train, but the lights were on and I saw no one inside. I headed for the goods yard and then out to the shed, but as I reached it she appeared out of nowhere. She had been inside. I had never seen a woman look like that. She looked like the devil was after her.'

'I think she thought that it was. What did you do?'

'She came at me with such fury that I panicked. I grabbed her and threw her against the fence. She … hit her head.' Robert lowered his. 'On one of the support pillars.'

As Slim watched, the old man began to sob. Still drunk, he felt his anger rising. 'And what did you do then, Robert? Come on, no more lies. Where did you take her?'

'She was cold, I could feel no pulse. I panicked, and the first thing I thought about was that no one would be able to look after my boy if I went to prison. I had to get back to the passengers waiting inside, or someone might come looking for me, so there was only one thing I could do. I dragged her body to the freight train. The closest freight wagon was beside the shed, the door unsecured. I dragged her body inside, shut the door, and then went back to the station office.' Robert fell quiet. He closed his eyes, pinching the bridge of his nose between his thumb and forefinger. His chest shook with a sudden gulping sob, and Slim wondered if he would be able to say anything else.

'What did you do, Robert?' he asked in barely more than a whisper. 'Tell me.'

Robert sighed. 'As soon as I possibly could, I gave the order for the freight train to depart.'

56

CHARLES BOSWORTH LOOKED NO HAPPIER TO SEE SLIM at such a late hour than Slim felt having walked, with a growing headache, halfway across Holdergate, but the old man opened the door and let him in anyway.

'What's going on, Slim? You don't look well. Do you have any idea what time it is? Christ, you look like I used to feel on Monday mornings.'

As a smirk appeared on Bosworth's lips, Slim lost it. He swung a fist into the old man's face and stepped back as Bosworth crumpled at his feet.

'There's more evidence to convict you of assaulting a former police officer than there is for pulling Robert Downs up for murder,' Bosworth said, scowling as he pressed a bag of frozen peas to his face. 'I thought you were ex-army? You punch like a pansy.'

Slim shrugged. 'I sank a bottle of whisky before I went round to see that murdering bastard.'

'Well, if you screw as badly as you fight, I can see why your wife left you.'

The clock read ten past midnight. Both men had a glass of amber in front of them, Bosworth's significantly larger, 'To help with the pain.'

'You told me you didn't know the boy's name. I got told Tom Jedder, which confused him with an unfortunate figure from local history. But Tom Edward said by someone with a speech impediment can come out sounding that way, can't it? The boy suffered from a facial deformity, so he might have had one, and an old man who used to put out food for Thomas's dog had one, too. You must have known, but you lied to me.'

Bosworth rubbed his eyes. 'Come on, Slim, give me a little leeway here. Bob Downs is an old friend, one of the oldest I've got. And he's a good man, despite what you might think. Bob went through hell and back when his wife topped herself, and he was as good a father as anyone could have been to that poor little boy. People not close to Bob, tourists, commuters, and the like, knew the boy as Tom Jedder, and that kept him disassociated from Bob's family. Bob had to put up with enough whispers behind his back already, yet he looked after that lad and he worked his backside off as station master. Out of respect for him I kept Thomas's death low-key. Despite what rumours and lies might have floated around at the time, it was an accident, witnessed both by the train driver and the guard. It had to go to the press, but I managed to keep the details quiet. Even if what you say is true, I still can't believe Bob had anything to do with Jennifer's disappearance.'

'He confessed to killing her.'

Bosworth shook his head. 'He's an old man, not in the best of health. Perhaps he made a mistake. You said he put her on the freight train? Impossible. We searched that freight train the following day, Slim. It was in a goods yard at Stafford station. There was no sign of Jennifer's body or that one had ever been on board.'

Slim sat back, frustrated. 'Then what happened to her? Where did she go?'

Bosworth waved the bag of peas in the air like a flag of surrender. 'That's what we've been wondering for the last forty-two years.'

57

SLIM'S BAGS WERE PACKED. CHARLES BOSWORTH HAD told him to call if he ever found a body, but they had parted on less than amiable terms after their abrasive final meeting. Having been seen to the door by Robert Downs with a regretful but confident, 'It was a long, long time ago. If the police wanted me, they'd have come by now', he prepared to leave Holdergate feeling more angry and frustrated than ever. He had come so close, but at the very last, Jennifer Evans's fate had eluded him.

With his head aching from a lingering hangover, Slim walked to Holdergate Station. On the way, he tried to call Lia, but the girl didn't answer. Slim was quietly glad; he wasn't sure what he'd say to her. She knew he was leaving and he had planned to call her from his office when he returned, to see if there was some way they could continue their relationship. An hour and a half by train between them was less than many commutes, but it wasn't the only barrier. There was the difference in age, and Slim's drinking. Lia might be better off without him after all.

He boarded a train, then got off at Manchester

214

Piccadilly half an hour later and made his way through the station to catch his connecting train. Looking up at the departures board, though, something caught his eye.

His own train was delayed, not due to arrive for another forty five minutes. However, a smaller commuter train was due to leave in just five minutes' time. The name of the destination station was like a tingle of hope, like finding a last drop at the bottom of a bottle.

Stafford.

It wasn't the direction he needed to go, but it wouldn't hurt to go a few stops out of his way, just to have a look. It might give him closure of a certain kind to see where Jennifer's trail finally went cold.

He made his way through the station to the correct platform and climbed on to the waiting train. There were few passengers. Slim took a seat near the back, his case pulled into the spare seat beside him. Despite his excitement, he was dozing when the train pulled in to Stafford, sleeping off the last of his hangover. He disembarked the train and made his way out onto the concourse where he sought out the information desk.

Announcing himself as a train enthusiast, it wasn't hard to find a member of staff willing to take him out to the goods yard for a look at some of the trains. Like the old man at Manchester Piccadilly, the amiable worker was more than happy to lead Slim across the tracks to the area where freights would have waited until the main platform was clear for unloading. Soon, Slim was standing within a few yards of what might have once been the end of Jennifer's personal journey. The trail for a pretty young nurse, wife, and mother ended here, among metal rails, gravel, and wooden sleepers.

'What happened to you?' Slim wondered aloud, just

out of hearing range of the station worker. He kicked at some weeds, frustrated that after everything he had no final, conclusive answer to tell Elena, who had put so much faith in his ability. He lifted his head, looking skyward for inspiration.

And paused, frowning.

Surely not, it was impossible.

But what if…?

He stared, unable to believe his eyes. Suddenly everything made sense.

'I'm sorry, I have to go,' he called to the office worker, and then turned and ran for the station.

58

LIA DROVE. SLIM HADN'T EVEN KNOWN SHE HAD A CAR, but now that he did, he was amazed it wasn't a scuffed mess with her violent, wayward style of driving. In the back, he hung on for all he was worth as she roared through blind hairpins and around overgrown corners, taking a route of her own making rather than following the one he had suggested on the map that now sat discarded on the seat beside him.

In the front passenger seat, Elena cried the whole way. Even when they pulled up at their destination, and despite Slim's assurances that it wasn't all a cruel lie, she held a handkerchief all the way to the top of the steps leading into St Mary's Priory, enclosed community for women. The crucifix positioned on its upper reaches was visible above the graffiti-laden wall that lined the goods yard at Stafford station.

Slim and Lia watched through the side windows as a woman in a grey and black nun's habit appeared from a door at the top to meet her. After a brief consultation, the woman waved Elena through the door, and the pair of them disappeared inside.

'It'll be all right now, won't it?' Lia asked, wiping a tear from her eye as she turned to Slim.

He nodded. 'I think so, yes.'

Lia smiled and gave a little shake of her head. 'Excuse my French, but how the hell did you manage to pull that off?'

Slim shrugged. 'A little bit of luck, I think.'

'Well, however you figured it out, you'll never cease to amaze me. Coffee?'

He nodded. 'Make it two. They'll need a while, I think.'

Elena, understandably, had looked uncertain when she opened the door to find Slim standing on her doorstep, soaking wet after the heavens had suddenly opened during his walk over to her place. Even so, it was hard to keep a smile off his face as he asked if she could spare him a couple of minutes.

'Mr. Hardy … every time I see you I expect it to be the last time … and then you show up again to disappoint me one more time.'

'Mrs. Trent, I apologise for everything that's happened, but this time I really do have some news. I'll get straight to the point. I've found your mother.'

Elena's face changed from shock to elation then to sorrow.

'Oh. Well, I'm really … I'm not sure what to say. You've found her body?'

Slim had wanted to deliver the news somberly, because

there was still much to uncover, but he couldn't stop himself breaking out in a wide smile.

'No,' he said, shaking his head, feeling a little tear of happiness beading in his eye. 'Your mother is very much alive, and considering her age, in very good health.'

~

'She must have literally thought the devil had come for her,' Slim said, wincing as he sipped the cinnamon latte which had been Lia's recommendation. 'She saw Bettelman and Thomas Downs peering through the fence. She ran back through the station, out into the goods yard where she found that shed and decided to hide. When she heard Robert approaching she thought she had been found. She attacked the figure as it opened the door, but got knocked unconscious. Robert was no medic and Jennifer was cold from being outside, so I can kind of understand why he thought she might be dead. However, I can only imagine what was going through her head that night as she lay in the dark, perhaps concussed, perhaps still unconscious. And when she crawled out of that freight carriage the next morning, the first thing she saw was the crucifix high on the wall of the priory outside the goods yard.'

Lia took a deep breath. 'Do you think they can create a new relationship?'

Slim shrugged. 'When I visited the priory I found myself face to face with an old woman who resembled the pictures Elena gave me. I called her by her name and I knew from her reaction I was right. She tried to deflect my questions at first, but when I produced a picture of Elena she relented. We talked a while. She said she always planned to go back, but a week became a month, then a year, then it became too late. She gave her life over to the church, but understood she had a past which might one day find her. She was open to meeting her daughter, and I think that the passage of years might have changed her somewhat. As for Elena, I think at this stage, she'll take what she can get.'

Lia nodded. She stared at Slim until he looked away.

'It's remarkable, that's all I can say. And you, Slim … you don't give up easily, do you?'

'No. It's proved a curse on more than one occasion. There are still a few things I need to do, though. I have to talk to Toby, explain a few things I found out. Whether he'll believe me or not, I don't know, but it might help him come to terms with a few things. And I'm looking forward to making a phone call to Charles Bosworth. Robert Downs might be off a murder charge, but he certainly obstructed justice during the original investigation. Believe it or not, I don't wish the old man ill. I think he made a bad mistake, but there's no doubting his actions altered the course of someone's life. However, I'd like to think both Jennifer and Elena would be forgiving.'

Lia nodded. She looked away for a moment, then looked back and gave Slim a small smile. 'And what about something else … what about us?'

Slim met her eyes. 'Well, you know I don't give up easily, and I think you've proved you don't give up easily either. If it's okay by you, I'd like to see what happens.'

'And enjoy whatever that is,' Lia said.

Slim reached across the table to take her hands in his. 'I think that's as good a place to start as any,' he said.

ABOUT THE AUTHOR

Jack Benton is a pen name of Chris Ward, the author of the dystopian *Tube Riders* series, the horror/science fiction *Tales of Crow* series, and the *Endinfinium* YA fantasy series, as well as numerous other well-received stand alone novels.

Slow Train is the fourth volume in the Slim Hardy mystery series.

Chris would love to hear from you:
chrisward@amillionmilesfromanywhere.net

ACKNOWLEDGMENTS

Big thanks as always to those of you who provided help and encouragement. My proofreaders and fact checkers Nick, Jenny, and Lisa, and the guys at The Cover Collection get a special heads up, as does as always, my muse, Jenny Twist.

In addition, extra thanks goes to my Patreon supporters, in particular to Amaranth Dawe, Charles Urban, Janet Hodgson, Juozas Kasiulis, Leigh McEwan, Teri L. Ruscak, James Edward Lee, Catherine Crispin, Christina Matthews, Alan MacDonald, Eda Ridgeway, and Jennie Brown.

You guys are awesome.

Made in the USA
Middletown, DE
05 February 2024